# Martha's Rough Season

Written by Bekah O'Brien
Illustrated by Bethany O'Brien

## Dedication:
This book is dedicated first of all to the Lord and Savior of all who put their trust in Him! These stories would be nothing without Him!

Secondly, this book is dedicated to my two brothers. They are such wonderful young men of God and I am proud to be their older sister!

## Isaiah 43:2
*When thou passest through the waters, I will be with thee; and through the rivers, they shall not overflow thee: when thou walkest through the fire, thou shalt not be burned; neither shall the flame kindle upon thee.*

## Lamentations 3:22-26
*It is of the LORD's mercies that we are not consumed, because his compassions fail not. They are new every morning: great is thy faithfulness. The LORD is my portion, saith my soul; therefore will I hope in him. The LORD is good unto them that wait for him, to the soul that seeketh him. It is good that a man should both hope and quietly wait for the salvation of the LORD.*

**The Knight Family:**
*Peter Knight, (Dad)*
*Rosemary Knight, (Mom)*
*Children:*
*Martha Knight, (age 13)*
*Thomas Knight, (age 11)*
*Twins: James Knight, (age 9)*
*Anna Knight, (age 9)*
*Lydia Knight, (age 5)*
*Sarah Knight, (age 4)*
*Elizabeth Knight, (age 2)*

# Chapters:

# Chapter 1
## Packing for a Move

Martha Knight packed the final books into a box, sealed it, and carried it downstairs and set it with all the other boxes stacked here and there around the living room. She sighed and looked around. Their home was looking less and less like home every day. She went back upstairs to her room to continue the process of packaging up their things. She felt a tug on her skirt; it was her sister Sarah.

"Don't forget my dolly, Martha," her sister reminded her, handing her rag doll upwards toward Martha with both hands.

"I won't," replied Martha, taking the doll from her sister's hands and placing it in the bottom of the box.

Martha finished packing and went downstairs to help her mother with supper. "Mom, what do you want me to do?"

"You could cut the bread and butter it for me."

"All right." Martha cut the bread in very thin slices, because they were trying to use as little flour as possible and save the rest for their trip to Colorado.

When Martha was done buttering the bread, she handed the plates and silverware to Lydia and Anna and they started to set the table. Martha looked up at the calendar on the kitchen wall. Today was March 25th. "Three weeks left," Martha sighed and helped her sisters with the table.

Five minutes later, everyone sat down at the table and bowed their heads to pray. "Dear Father in Heaven," prayed Dad, "thank You so much for all You've given us. We don't deserve anything. Lord, please bless us and protect us on our upcoming journey. Father, we don't want to leave our home here, but we feel that it is Your will. Please help us to accept it without question. We love You. In Jesus' name we pray, amen."

Everyone dug into the meal of meat and bread. Mom started the conversation, "The books have all been packed away, thanks to Martha. Next, I'll need to start packing all the delicate and sentimental items in the house."

"You're making progress, Rosemary," complemented Dad.

"Yes, slowly but surely; Martha," she turned to her eldest daughter, "I'll need you to play outside tomorrow afternoon with your sisters. I would prefer them not to be running around when I pack the delicate things. It will only be for a little while. I'm going to dust and polish them, and if everything goes well, I should finish it within an hour. I was thinking you could take them out to the barn."

"Sure, Mom," replied Martha.

"Me want to see animals!" exclaimed Elizabeth, clapping her hands with delight.

"Well, if you promise me you won't cause Martha any trouble, I'll let you go instead of taking a nap."

"Me no cause twouble, Mummy," Elizabeth said, laughing.

Once everyone was finished with the meal, Martha helped clear the dishes away and wash them. After the dishes were done, Dad came up to her and handed her a letter. "I found this waiting at the post office when I went to town today."

"Thanks, Dad," Martha replied, grasping the letter with her hands.

"You're welcome. Once you finish, come downstairs for devotions."

"Yes, Dad," replied Martha.

Martha rushed to her room, plopped down upon the bed and opened the letter; it read:

*March 17th, 1931*

*Dear Martha,*

*I'm glad to hear of the news that you and your family will be moving here! My dad told me before you probably knew, but he asked me not to say anything. I'm excited that we will live close to each other so we'll be able to visit often. I know you are probably very upset to hear that you'll be leaving your friends, and you are probably discouraged. I know it's hard but hang in there. I'll be praying for you, that your faith in the Lord will stay stronger than ever!*

*I think you'll make fast friends with the ones I have here. I know it won't seem like home to you, but maybe after a little while it will. Libby and Bealle are already asking questions about you and your younger sisters like: "What are they like? What do they look like? What are their interests? Will we like the same things?" I try to be patient with them and answer all their questions, but sometimes I do get impatient with their constant prattle.*

*Martha, I can't wait until you and your family arrive. Please know that I'm praying for you during this rough time. I try to remind myself constantly that my joy in your moving here is not your same feeling.*

*I love you!*

*Your Sister in Christ,*
*Irene Williams*

Martha folded the letter back up, put it on her desk and sighed, she doubted that she could ever call any place but here "home", again.

---------

The next morning, as Martha and Anna were doing the breakfast dishes, Anna asked, "Does Irene have any siblings?"

"Yes, she does. She has an older and younger brother and twin sisters, Libby and Bealle, who are not too much older than you. They're eleven."

"I wonder what they'll be like? Will they like us?"

"I'm sure they have the same questions about us."

"Oh, Martha, I don't want to leave. I'd rather stay here."

9

Martha put an arm around her sister. "I know it's hard. I wish we didn't have to leave either, but we need to trust God that He'll work everything out in His time, and in His way. All we can do is wait patiently."

"I know, but sometimes it's really hard."

"I agree that it is hard. It's because we're human; we want everything to happen 'our way' and not God's way."

"I'll try to wait patiently," replied Anna as she put her apron away and went to wait for morning family devotions.

After devotions, Martha took her sisters out to the barn to play so her mom could get her packing done.

"I hope the snow goes away soon. I'm ready for all the flowers to pop out. Look!  There are some daffodils to greet us," said Anna, hurrying to go and pick the flowers.

"Oh, Anna! Don't pick them. Let them stay there; we can enjoy them longer."

"But can't I pick even one? Just to remember this home? I would like to press it and keep it forever!" asked Anna, politely.

"All right. Just one, though."

Anna picked the flower and hurried back to the house to put it in her room to press it in a book. She was hurrying down the upstairs hall when Mom came out from her room with a vase in her hand. Anna bumped into her and the vase crashed to the floor. Mom became very upset.

"Anna, you were supposed to be outside. That was my grandmother's vase that you made me drop, and it was very dear to me. Go outside at once!"

Anna had tears in her eyes and was sorry that she caused so much trouble. "I'm so sorry, Mom. I didn't mean to run into you. I should have been acting more lady-like. I'm sorry."

"I forgive you; now go out to the barn now and don't return until Martha's with you, all right?"

"Yes, ma'am," she replied weakly.

Once Anna got to the barn again, she told her story and Martha expressed sympathy for her, but told her gently that next time she should walk instead of run.

"I will next time. I promise," Anna whimpered.

The girls played with Nellie, their dog, and Jubiliee, Martha's kitten. Martha had brought some paper and a pencil to work on her next letter to Irene, which she would mail when they were leaving Helena, Montana.

*March 25th, 1931,*

*Dear Irene,*

*Thank you for your prayers. This will be my last letter until we meet face-to-face again. It will be VERY hard to leave my friends, but I'm trying to trust God completely with my needs. I'm excited to see you and meet your friends, but I'm not sure if I could feel that any place could be my home again. I feel really strange. I'm almost afraid to look forward to liking Colorado so much that I'll forget my first home. I'm very confused right now.*

*I'm trying to stay strong for my siblings. My tear wells seem to have run dry on me, for I have shed not one tear since the dreaded day I found out that we would be moving. But yet, I feel it needs to all come out. I think crying is God's way of relief, but I can't seem to find any. When will these strange feelings end? I don't know!*

*Keep me in your prayers!*

*Your sister in Christ,*

*Martha Knight*

Martha sealed the letter and watched her sisters play with Jubilee for a bit. Then, when an hour-and-a-half had passed, Martha decided they should make their way to the house once again. Anna decided she would stay out and play with Nellie some more. Martha guessed there was more to it but didn't say anything and walked to the house with her other three sisters.

Martha entered from the back door and saw that her mom was hard at work making lunch. Martha settled Lydia and Sarah with a puzzle and Elizabeth with a picture book while she helped Mom with the meal.

As Martha entered the kitchen, Mom looked at her daughter and asked, "Where's Anna? Didn't she come in with you?"

"No, she wanted to stay and play with Nellie some more," replied Martha, taking off her coat and letting Jubilee in the back door.

"Oh, I need to go out and talk to her. Will you stir this soup for me, please?"

"Sure," replied Martha, taking the spoon from her hand.

Mom got her coat and buttoned it all the way and made her way to the barn. As she opened the door, she found Anna playing tug of war with Nellie with an old piece of rope.

"Anna," started Mom, "I'm sorry I lost my self-control. I didn't mean to, but I was upset about the vase. I should've had more self-control, and I will try to do better next time. When I said I forgave you, I really didn't. I was still angry in my heart. But I do forgive you now. Would you please forgive me?"

"Oh, Mom, I forgive you! You had every right to be upset and mad. I'm sorry I went into the house and disobeyed you. Will you forgive me?"

"Yes, I already have. Come on, let's go to the house and eat lunch."

"All right, Mom."

So, hand-in-hand, mother and daughter walked to the house.

# Chapter 2
## Late Delivery

March 27th, 1931, a wagon drove up the Knight's driveway. Martha was coming from the barn, and she saw it was Leslie McShire. Martha hurried up and asked, "Is anything wrong, Mrs. McShire?"

"Is your mom here?"

"Yes, let me go get her."

Martha went inside and told Mom that their friend was outside. Mom dried her hands on her apron and went out on the porch. "What is it, Leslie? Is everything all right?"

"Michael Share stopped by my house a short ago and said that Janelle has gone into labor. I'm on my way there now. Would you accompany me? I may need some help with the delivery."

"Sure. Let me grab my coat first."

Mom came back out a minute later and said to Martha, "Watch the children for me."

"All right."

Martha went back into the house as she watched her mother and Mrs. McShire speed off. Lydia came up to her big sister and asked, "Martha, where is Mommy going?"

"Mrs. Share is going to have her baby, and Mrs. McShire wanted Mommy to go with her."

"Okay," Lydia replied and went back to playing with Elizabeth.

Martha decided she needed to make some lunch, so she went into kitchen and started preparing sandwiches and she started praying, *Dear Lord, please help the birth to go well, and please bless the Share's with a healthy baby. Amen.*

----------

Later that evening, the McShire's wagon slowly pulled up, and Martha went to see her mom. Mom hopped out of the wagon, said a few words to Leslie, then she turned and walked up the steps to the house. Martha realized her mom was tired so she had her sit down and rest. "How did it go?"

"Fine. It was just a long wait. The baby wasn't born until four o'clock but everything went fine. Praise the Lord."

"Well, don't keep me in suspense. What's the gender? Boy or girl?"

"They had a healthy baby girl. Her name is Janelle Leigh Share, 8 pounds, 6 ounces."

"Oh, I'm so glad. So, Janelle after her mother?"

"Yes, Michael insisted upon it, so they decided to name her Janelle and call her Jana, for short."

"How cute."

"Mrs. Share is really tired. Michael asked if you would come and take care of Jana while Mrs. Share rests for a few days until she gets her strength back, since you've had experience with babies."

"Sure, I'd be glad to help. When does she want me?"

"As soon as you can--I was thinking first thing tomorrow morning."

"Sure, that would work fine for me. I'll go and pack, and I think I'll go ahead and get some sleep. I have a feeling that tomorrow's going to be a long day."

"Okay, that's probably a good idea. Goodnight."

"Goodnight."

----------

The next morning after breakfast, Dad dropped Martha off at the Share home. After a few words with Michael, he drove home to get to work on the chores.

Michael led Martha to her room and said, "You get settled in and then you can come downstairs to meet the baby. Janelle is nursing Jana right now, but she should be almost finished."

"Okay, Mr. Share. Thanks. Congratulations on your new little one."

"Thanks, Martha," replied Mr. Share with a proud smile.

Martha put her clothes in the closet and put her hair brush and other necessities on the dresser. Then, after taking off her coat and hanging it up in the closet, she went down the hall and into the living room, where the proud father was sitting on the couch with his little baby girl in his arms. Martha came and stood looking over his shoulder.

"She's darling."

Jana Share was sleeping peacefully in her father's arms. She had rosy little round cheeks with a little bit of black hair on her head, which was a characteristic of her father, whose short, wavy black hair matched that of his daughter's. She had her mother's little, well-shaped nose and chin.

"May I hold her?" asked Martha softly.

"Sure, come sit here beside me and I'll let you hold her."

Martha sat down, and Mr. Share put Jana gently into her arms. "Oh, it's been forever since I held a little one this small in my arms." Martha gasped as she felt Jana move gently.

"Yes, she's a miracle from her hair down to her little toes."

"I'm sure. She is definitely a blessing from God."

"She is indeed! Well, I need to go out to the barn to milk the cow."

"Yes, sir, Jana and I will be fine. I'll take good care of her."

"I know you will."

Martha played gently with the baby's little hands and cooed to her. Jana just kept sleeping peacefully.

After a little while, Martha carried her into her mother's room, where Mrs. Share was reading a book. She looked up when Martha entered. "So, how do you like my baby?" Mrs. Share asked, smiling.

"She's wonderful! How are you feeling?"

"Tired, but wonderful. I can't believe that she's finally here. I could feel her in my womb for so long, but now she's finally here. Oh, she's just a miracle and gift from God. I'll never forget her first cry when she was just born. She's just wonderful."

"I'm SO happy for you. She was a late baby, wasn't she?"

"Yes, she certainly was."

"Well, I guess it doesn't matter now that she's here," replied Martha, smiling at her friend and placing Jana in her bassinet.

"Martha, would you move her bassinet into the living room so she doesn't disturb me when I sleep?"

"Sure." She handed Jana back to her mom, and Martha carried the bassinet into the living room. Martha came back and gently lifted her out of her mother's arms which caused a little whimper from Jana, but she soon calmed down again.

Martha gently laid her once again in her bassinet, made sure she was swaddled tightly enough, and then went to see if Mrs. Share needed anything.

"Would you bring me a glass of water? There should be some in the ice box," replied Janelle in answer to her question.

"Certainly," replied Martha, going to the ice box and getting the desired drink. After Janelle had had her fill, Martha helped her lie down so she could rest. She shut the door and made her way to the kitchen to prepare some lunch for Mr. Share and herself.

--------

As Martha plunked the lunch dishes into the sink, Jana started to fuss. *I wonder what she needs? Perhaps a diaper change?*

She walked over to the cradle where Jana had worked her tiny arm free of her blanket that tightly swaddled her. She started to scratch her face. "Oh no, Miss Jana," Martha softly cooed to her, "you can't do that to your face, you'll scratch it up."

She felt the end of the baby's gown and took note of Jana's wet diaper. Setting her on the changing table, she quickly and efficiently changed her diaper. All the while, little Jana looked up at her with her shiny blue eyes.

"We're almost done now," Martha talked to the baby, "I'm just going to put a pair of your tiny little socks onto your hands so that you don't scratch up your pretty little face."

Martha chose a pair of adorable, little pink socks, and just like her parents had done with Elizabeth and the others, gently eased them over Jana's tightly bound up fists. After finishing, she took the baby and laid her back down in her bassinet after rocking her to sleep.

After peeking in at Mrs. Share and finding that she was still sleeping, Martha went to cleaning the living room while Jana was sleeping.

At two o'clock, Jana was ready for her feeding, so Martha woke up Mrs. Share and told her that Jana was fussing. She then laid Jana in her arms so she could eat and went to start preparing supper.

----------

Later that night, Martha made sure that Jana was okay, and seeing that she was, went upstairs to bed. After her prayers were said, she slid under the covers and fell fast asleep.

About two o'clock in the morning, Martha heard something. She sat up and wondered where she was for a second, but then remembered that she was at the Share's home, helping take care of Jana.

The thirteen-year-old realized that the baby was crying. She slipped out of bed, put her robe and slippers on and went downstairs. Martha changed her diaper, but Jana was still upset. "Martha," she heard a voice quietly calling her name from where Janelle was sleeping.

Martha walked quietly over with Jana crying in her arms. "Yes? Sorry if Jana woke you. I'm trying to calm her down."

"No, it's okay. It's her feeding time anyway. If you'll bring her to me, I'll feed her real quick. You can go back to bed. I'll put her back in the bassinet." replied Janelle, sleepily.

"All right, are you sure you don't want me to stay up and put her back for you?"

"No, it's fine. I'll see you in the morning."

"Okay, thanks, Mrs. Share. See you in the morning."

Martha went back to her bedroom, snuggled under the covers and sighed contentedly, this was good practice for being a mother.

----------

The three days passed quickly, and before Martha knew it, she was saying goodbye to the Shares.

"Thank you so much for your help while my wife was recovering, Martha, I appreciate it," exclaimed Mr. Share.

"You're most welcome. It was my pleasure. It was good practice for me," replied Martha, kissing Jana on the forehead before stepping into the wagon.

"Thanks again, Martha," said Mr. Share, waving as the wagon started forward.

"Goodbye!"' called Martha.

## Chapter 3
## Goodbyes and Heartache

April 14th was a Sunday and the last day the Knight family would be in their home.

"Martha, would you tie this bow in my hair?" asked Anna.

"Sure," replied Martha, doing as her sister requested. "Are you ready to leave for church?"

"Yes. I just have to get my Bible."

"Good. After you get it, come out and get in the wagon."

"Yes, Martha," replied Anna, hurrying to get the desired item.

Martha put her sweater on and buttoned it. It was still chilly, but most of the cold weather had passed.

Martha stepped out the door and into the wagon, pulling Elizabeth onto her lap for the ride. A minute later, the wagon started for church. It seemed everybody was holding their breath and enjoying this one last ride to church. Mom had secretly put a few small hankies in her purse in case there were any tears, which she was sure there would be.

They arrived at church and Martha helped her younger sisters get seated on their pew and then, with her parents' permission, went to talk with her friends. She found them in a corner, and Cathryn Williams turned toward her and gave her a hug. "We're going to miss you! We'll just make the best out of this last Sunday."

"Yes," agreed the other girls.

"I heard the boys talking about setting up a game of kick ball after church. You always enjoyed that game. Will you play with us?"

"Sure. I'd love to," replied Martha.

"It looks as if Pastor Share is ready to start the service. See you later," called Cathryn.

"Please turn to number 648 in your hymnals." said Pastor Share, as he flipped to the number himself.

*"Saviour, like a shepherd lead us,*
*Much we need Thy tender care;*
*In Thy pleasant pastures feed us,*
*For our use Thy folds prepare.*

*Blessed Jesus, Blessed Jesus,*
*Thou hast bought us, Thine we are;*
*Blessed Jesus, blessed Jesus,*
*Thou has bought us, Thine we are."*

After the service was concluded, Martha went to talk with her friends. They chose a table to sit at and everyone was quiet for a bit, not sure what to say to comfort their friend.

"You'll like my cousin's family a lot. They're a bunch of fun. I've never met Trevor, but Libby and Bealle are real funny and look exactly alike," exclaimed Rose Williams.

"I'm sure I'll have fun with them."

"We'll all be praying for you. I know it will be hard," said Polly.

"Thank you. I'm going to try my hardest to keep my eyes focused on the Lord, and try to trust His will for my life, although I can't see it yet. But I guess that's normally the way it is."

"Yes," the others agreed.

Francesca's forehead furrowed as she thought. *Why does Martha have such a good attitude? She's moving away from everything and everyone, yet, she says that she's doing her best to trust God. She isn't feeling sorry for herself or looking for self-pity...like I did when I first moved here. Is that the difference? Martha's trusting God and not looking for self-pity from others?*

Martha noticed her friend's unusual quietness and touched her arm lightly. "Francesca? Are you okay?"

"Hmm? Oh, yes. I'm fine."

"Are you sure?"

"Yes. I'm fine, really."

"Let's go and get our food," suggested Mary Poltor.

"Okay. I can't wait to play kick ball later today," replied Martha.

---------

"Okay, you're up to kick, Martha," called Bruce Gates, who was their captain for kick ball.

"All right," replied Martha, going up to home plate. She took a deep breath and focused on the ball. Wham! The ball flew into the air and Martha made a run for it. She made it to second base. Rose was up next. She made an out. Martha sucked in her breath. "That's only the first out. We can make it. Come on, Anna!" she cheered as her sister came up to kick.

Anna kicked and made it to first base and Martha to third. Fred Gates was up next. Fred kicked a home run which caused a 3-0 lead for Martha's team. The next two to kick both made outs so it was the other team's turn to kick.

Benjamin McShire was the other team's captain and he kicked first. He made it to third base in one kick. Martha shifted nervously on her feet; they were going to have to play hard to beat this team.

Polly was up after her big brother, Benjamin, and Martha watched her friend focus intensely on the ball as it was hurled toward her.

"Come on, sis!" called Benjamin, encouraging his sister.

As if in slow motion, Polly stepped forward and kicked the ball. It didn't make it very far, but she was able to make it to first base, allowing Benjamin to score a point for his team as his foot hit home plate.

Martha watched as Timothy Williams was up to kick next. *It's 3-1. I wonder how many more they'll score before the inning is over?*

Timothy kicked vigorously but swung his leg too hard and missed the ball. Martha felt a bit bad for him, noticing his embarrassment, but Cathryn, who was on Martha's team, cheered for her brother. "It's okay, Tim! Try again!"

Martha smiled at her friend. Cathryn, his sister, did the right thing. No matter who won, they wanted to make sure that everyone had a good time.

Timothy kicked again, and, though he didn't hit the ball, it was a much more careful kick. "Come on, Tim! You can do it!" cried Rose this time.

Timothy looked hard at the ball as Samuel pitched it again carefully towards him. The seven-year-old made contact with the ball this time and it sailed over the kickball 'diamond' and he made a run for it. He made it to second base, sending Polly home.

*It's 3-2 now...,* Martha mused to herself inwardly.

The next kicker struck out. The second kicker, Billy, made it to second base and Martha cringed as she watched Timothy slide to home base.

It was a tied game.

Samuel struck out the next two kickers and it was Martha's team's turn to kick.

*All right, Martha, let's show them what we're made of.* The competitive thirteen-year-old stepped up to kick.

"Come on, Martha, you can do it!" cheered Anna.

Martha gave a thumbs-up to her sister and focused on the pitcher.

At the end of the game, it was six to four. Martha's team lost, but they still had had a great time. They congratulated Benjamin's team and then went in for dessert.

----------

Before Martha knew it, it was time to say goodbye to her friends.

"Promise us you'll write soon!" said Polly.

"Yes, I'll write all of you as often as I can."

"We'll miss you!" said Cathryn. "More than we can say."

"I'm going to miss all of you, too. I don't want to leave, but I guess this is what God has for me and my family right now."

"Martha, look at it this way, God's just giving you another adventure. Just accept the challenge and see what He does with your life. If it's His will, we'll see you again," said Cathryn.

"Oh, you're the greatest friends anyone could ask for!"

"We'll miss you. I see your father waving you over. It's time to go," replied Cathryn.

"Bye!" Martha waved and hurried to join her family.

"Wait, Martha!" called Francesca as Martha was almost to the door.

"Yes, Francesca? Are you well? You're as white as a sheet!"

"Martha, whatever you have, I want it."

"What?!"

"That peace that you seem to always have, I want it."

"Oh, Francesca, I'm so glad! All you have to do is trust in the Lord Jesus, and you will be saved."

"But how?"

"Just ask Him. Tell Him you want to receive His ultimate gift. Do you want me to pray with you?"

"Yes! Oh, yes! Please."

Then, let me go and tell my dad that really quickly so that he'll know where I am and we'll find a private place that's away from the crowd.

A few minutes later, the two girls had found a quiet place. Martha and Francesca bowed their heads and prayed, and a few minutes later, Francesca was a Daughter of the King!

"Where shall I read to learn how to grow in my relationship with Jesus?" asked Francesca.

"Why don't you start reading in the Book of John and then go from there?"

"Okay. Thanks, Martha. I feel this joy in my heart. I'm going to go and tell the others. Thank you for praying with me. I'm going to miss you terribly. You were a sort of mentor for me, you know? You always were so kind to me when I was absolutely horrid. I'm sorry for the way I acted, would you please forgive me? I'm going to do my best to do better."

"Of course I forgive you, Francesca. I'm going to miss you too. We'll write often, and you can tell me how you are growing in the Lord."

"I will! Bye," replied Francesca, giving Martha one last hug and heading towards the others.

Martha sighed and looked around the building. This would be the last time she would be in the building for a very long time. She took a deep breath, then headed out to the wagon to tell her family the good news of Francesca's deliverance.

----------

Later that night, Martha got out her diary and wrote her last entry in the diary before they left.

*April 14th, 1931*

*Dear God,*

*Today is the last day that I will be at this home. I'm very sad. I do have some good news, though! Francesca Bear became a Christian at church today! I'm so glad. I knew she was hurting a lot from her move from Idaho to Montana. Thank You for helping me to be an example to her.*

*Lord, my heart aches terribly. I do NOT want to leave here, my home, my friends. Lord, when I think about it, it almost seems unbearable. But please help me to see this as another adventure. I can't wait to see what You have in store for me.*

*Martha Rosemary Knight*

# Chapter 4
## On the Road

It was a sad morning the next day. Martha didn't want to get out of bed, but she knew she must. Her feet touched the floor and she went to brush her hair and wash her face, saying to her younger sisters, "It's time to get up, girls."

"Is it time, already? What time is it?" asked Anna.

"Four o'clock."

"Oh, yes, we're leaving today," replied Anna, sighing.

"Come on out of bed and I'll help you dress."

"All right."

Martha woke her other sisters and helped them dress. Then, after dressing herself, she took Elizabeth by the hand and went downstairs to eat some cold biscuits. The family sat around the table for the last time.

"Dear Jesus," prayed Dad, "please bless us on our journey and get us to our new home safely. Please bless this home for the next family that lives here. May they find joy in You. Please nourish this food to our bodies and please bless the hands that made it; in Your Name alone, amen."

Everyone ate, trying to be cheerful. After the dishes were done and packed away, everyone got to work packing the last things into the wagon. Everyone went and looked around their house for the last time. Martha didn't believe this was their house anymore. The bare walls didn't speak of the fun, laughter, tears and memories that had passed through the home. Sarah clung to her dress, crying, "Why, oh why, do we have to leave? I want to stay here."

"I know, Sarah. I don't want to leave either, but cheer up and be a good girl for Daddy and Mommy. Can you be a brave girl for the next few months?"

"Yes, I think so," replied Sarah mournfully.

"Good girl. Now go out to the wagon; I'll be along shortly."

"All right, Martha," she replied and walked out of sight.

Martha breathed a last goodbye to her room and then went downstairs. Mom was crying softly, and Dad had his arm around her, leading her toward the wagon. The family gathered around on the front porch and prayed, and Dad read a verse: *"When thou passest through the waters, I will be with thee; and through the rivers, they shall not overflow thee: when thou walkest through the fire, thou shalt not be burned; neither shall the flame kindle upon thee."*

"Let's sing, 'What a Friend We have in Jesus,'" suggested Thomas.

> *"What a friend we have in Jesus,*
> *all our sins and griefs to bear,*
> *what a privilege to carry,*
> *everything to God in prayer, oh, what peace*
> *we often forfeit, oh, what needless pain we*
> *bear. All, because we do not carry,*
> *everything to God in prayer."*

After they finished the hymn, everyone got into the wagon and the journey began. Martha looked sadly at the white house they were leaving behind.

It would be a long while before she ever saw that house again. And what adventures she would have before then, she couldn't tell. But she could feel an empty feeling right in the middle of her chest, growing bigger and bigger with every inch they traveled. She just kept repeating that everything would work together, to them that love God, to them who are the called according to His purpose. Although, she had no clue of what that purpose was.

Four hours later, they arrived in town. Dad said that they would break for an early lunch there. So, driving the wagon to the edge of town, he helped Mom unpack the necessary things to make the meal. Martha helped her sisters down and then went to help Thomas get buckets of water from the creek.

"I can't wait to get to Colorado," exclaimed Thomas enthusiastically.

"I'm kind of excited too, but I really don't want to leave here," replied Martha.

"I know. I don't want to leave either. But I believe this is what God has for us right now and I'm looking forward to the adventure."

"Yes, I guess you're right." Martha stepped onto a log, dipped her bucket and filled it to the brim. She started to step back off when she began to lose her balance. "Thomas!" she screamed. Thomas whirled around, spilling half of his bucket, just in time to see his sister plunge into the water.

"Oh, the water's cold!" Martha shivered as she tried to get up. Thankfully, the water was shallow where she fell in, and with Thomas' hand, she was able to get out easily. Martha was shivering dreadfully; her clothes were sticking to her skin and her teeth were chattering so hard that she thought they would fall out. Thomas refilled the buckets and they both hurriedly walked back to the wagon. Mom stared at her daughter in bewilderment and asked, "What happened?"

"I-I f-fell into t-the c-c-creek."

"I should say so!" exclaimed Mom, wrapping a towel around her daughter and leading her by the fire to warm up."

After her teeth had stopped chattering some, Martha went into the wagon and changed into a dry dress and re-braided her hair. Ten minutes later, she stepped out of the wagon and joined her family for lunch.

Before moving on, Mom, Martha, and Lydia went to the store to pick up a few last minute things that they needed. As they entered the store, the bell over the door jingled and Martha smiled at Mr. Martin. "Hello, Mr. Martin."

"Hello, Martha. Is your family heading out to Colorado now?"

Martha nodded sadly.

"Well, I'll sure miss seeing your family around."

"We'll miss you, too," responded Martha.

"Me too!" piped up Lydia.

Mr. Martin smiled at the dark haired little girl as he took Mrs. Knight's order and began to fill it quickly.

As Mom handed Mr. Martin the correct amount of money, the storekeeper turned to Martha. "You know last fall, when you encouraged me to come back to Christ?"

Martha's eyes lit up as she nodded vigorously. "Yes."

"Well, I've done just that. I'm attending the church here in town. How can I ever thank you enough for what you said to me?"

Martha blushed at the praise. "It really wasn't me, sir. God gave me the words to say. I'm just so happy to hear that you have a restored relationship with Christ."

"Me too!" exclaimed the happy storekeeper.

The Knight's said goodbye and headed out to join the others to continue traveling. Martha prayed, *Thank You for using me to encourage Mr. Martin, and for the encouragement he just gave. Help me to always trust You, Lord!*

# Chapter 5
# Traveling

The Knight family traveled many days from sunup to sundown on their way to Colorado. When they would camp for the night, Martha would help her mom with supper, wash the dishes, and listen sleepily as Dad read devotions. Then she would get ready for bed, lay Elizabeth down in her bed and fall asleep herself.

The sleep Martha got didn't seem enough. She would get up at five o'clock and help Mom with breakfast, then go and help dress her sisters, and sit down to breakfast. After devotions were done, the family would start again on their journey at about six-thirty.

Mom, Martha, and the others would walk alongside the wagon to get some exercise until lunchtime. Then they would break and have lunch and Martha would ride in the wagon and read books and play puzzles with her sisters for the rest of the day. This was their daily routine.

On one such morning, Martha awoke to Mom calling her name, telling her to get up. "Is it time to get up already, Mom?"

"Yes, I'm afraid so."

"All right, but I'll tell you one thing, I'm going to sleep for days on end when we reach the Williams' home," Martha said with a smile.

Mom just laughed softly and went back to making oatmeal. Martha got up and dressed and ran down to get water from a nearby brook. As she knelt down on the bank to fill the bucket with water, she heard a rustling and a grunt. She looked up and about twenty five feet in front of her across the brook was a bear!

Martha slowly stood and swallowed down a scream. *What do I do? I don't want to scare it!*

Just then, she remembered something that her grandfather had told her. *Grandpa told me that if a bear sees me, I should move very slowly away, so I don't draw its attention to me. Although, he's probably already smelled me! God, please help me get away!*

Martha slowly backed away from the bear, and she watched in terror as it stood on its back legs and began to sniff the air. Martha looked behind her and saw the clearing in the trees. *God, help me to get back safely. Divert the bear's attention away from me, please!*

Soon, Martha found herself entering the clearing and as she noticed that the bear dropped on all fours again and looked away from her, she burst into a run.

Mom looked up from serving the oatmeal and asked, "What's the matter?"

"There's a-a bear..., back there across the stream."

"Is the bear behind you?"

"No, no I don't think so." Martha gingerly looked behind her.

"Well, you just wake up your sisters, and I'll send your father down to fetch the buckets. I'm glad you escaped unharmed."

"Me too," replied Martha, as she breathed a sigh of relief.

After breakfast was finished, the family had devotions and the wagon started forward on their journey again. Martha had Lydia and Sarah's hands, and Anna was with Mom and Elizabeth in the wagon.

"Martha, can't I go and sit in the wagon, my feet ache from doing so much walking," complained Lydia.

49

"Yes, you may, just try not to disturb Elizabeth. She didn't sleep so well last night, so she's sleeping in the wagon right now."

"I won't," and she ran and climbed up on the wagon.

Martha kept on walking and she had to admit that even her feet ached from walking so much, but she came to the conclusion that walking was good exercise for her and she plodded on.

Lunch time came around and Martha helped her mom make sandwiches, and before long, they were on the road again. Elizabeth wasn't sleepy after her morning nap, so Mom decided she could skip her afternoon one. Martha held Elizabeth on her lap and set to memorizing verses.

It wasn't even two hours after they left their spot for lunch when Elizabeth started to fuss. Martha tried singing to her to help her go to sleep, but she didn't seem to be sleepy. Martha felt her head to make sure she didn't have a fever. Thankfully, she didn't and Martha breathed a sigh of relief, but then she noticed the spots on her sister's arm. She gasped and called to Dad to stop the wagon.

When the wagon stopped, Martha called her mother down to come and take a look at Elizabeth.

After examining her, Mom pronounced that she had poison ivy. Mom whipped up some cream and rubbed it on her skin and that seemed to help some, but Elizabeth now seemed to be hot and feverish.

Martha held Elizabeth while the wagon continued on and muttered to herself in dismay, "This is going to be a long day."

----------

By four-o'clock, Elizabeth was still cranky and now she was crying. Martha's ears hurt from all the wailing but she endured it until they finally stopped to camp for that night.

Martha kept holding Elizabeth while Mom prepared supper. She ate in the wagon with Elizabeth. Finally, after Mom replenished the cream upon her arm, she got sleepy and fell to sleep in her sister's arms.

Martha laid her on a blanket and got ready for bed herself and lay beside her. She only hoped that she wouldn't contract the poison ivy, but the chances were that she probably would.

----------

The next morning, Martha felt miserable. She had indeed caught the poison ivy, and she got up and put the cream on her arms and went to fetch the water again.

Lydia and Sarah were both grumpy that day and Martha thought it was going to be a horrid day for her. She asked God to give her the strength to get through the day and started walking behind the wagon. With each step, her poison ivy seemed to itch more and more. She felt hot and clammy, and she just wanted to hop in the river to cool down the itching. She would have welcomed falling in the river now, she thought to herself with a little sarcastic laugh.

"My feet ache. I don't want to go anymore. Can't we rest today?" complained Sarah.

"Yeah, I'm so tired. I wish Dad would stop for a day," replied Lydia with her complaint.

Martha took a deep breath and said, "Well, the less we stop, the sooner we'll get to Colorado." Martha resisted the urge to itch her poison ivy and tried to sound cheerful, but thought it was a weak attempt.

"But Colorado is SO far away. Why couldn't we stay in Montana?" complained Sarah even more.

"I don't know why, Sarah, but we should do our best to trust God in everything."

"I know, but it's really hard and I'm losing my patience," exclaimed Lydia, kicking a stone as she walked.

Martha was getting impatient with her griping sisters. At least they didn't have poison ivy, but she replied calmly, "Well, let's forget about that and play a game."

"What game?"

"I spy, with my little eye, something that is...brown," started Martha.

Lydia looked around and said in return, "That tree trunk over there?"

"Yes, you're right."

Anna came over from where she was walking with Mom and joined in the game. "It's your turn, Sarah," said Martha.

"I spy, with my little eye, something that is...white..."

"The clouds?" guessed Anna.

"Right!" replied Sarah happily

Martha was glad that she could stop her sisters' complaining, but she still felt miserable herself and wanted to stop.

Finally, lunch came around and Martha helped her mom prepare the food, then, climbing into the wagon, plopped down on some quilts and fell into a hot, feverish sleep. She dreamed she was in the desert searching for water, but couldn't find any. She woke up with a start. She was sitting straight up and she seemed all sweaty. She slowly laid back down and breathed slowly. The air seemed thicker and it was harder to breath, and the next moment she was being shaken awake by Anna. "I must've fallen asleep again," said Martha to herself. "What is it, Anna?"

"It's time to get up and do chores. We've camped for the night."

Martha let out a groan, "I feel sick and itchy."

"Mom!" called Anna from the wagon, "Martha isn't feeling so good."

Mom hurriedly climbed into the wagon and placed a hand on her daughter's forehead. She was burning hot with fever!

"She must have done too much today with that poison ivy. I should have been keeping an eye on her. Anna, run and tell Thomas to go and fetch some water for me; I've got to get this fever down."

Anna went and did as she was told. The rash had spread all the way to Martha's neck and she groaned with aches. "Mom, I don't feel so good. I feel hot and itchy."

"I know, darling. I shouldn't have let you do so much today. I'm sorry."

Martha mumbled a reply and again laid back into sleep, but Mom shook her. "Martha, I need to change you into a nightgown, this dress is soaking wet from all your sweat."

Martha slowly sat up and got dressed in a nightgown. Shortly after, Thomas arrived with the water, and Anna came with some rags. Mom put the cold rags on her daughter's forehead and Martha sighed. "Oh, that feels SO good. I just want to be cool."

"Well, young lady, you'll be in bed for the next few days."

Martha looked disappointed but didn't say anything and fell into a peaceful sleep.

---------

The next afternoon, Martha was again feeling hot and feverish and Mom was worried about her. It hadn't gotten much better since the day before, and Mom asked Dad if they could afford a doctor the next time they arrived at a town. Dad consented and said the next town shouldn't be more than five miles ahead. Dad pushed Zoe and Vernon even harder to reach the next town before sunset.

As they arrived at the next town, Dad hitched up the horses to a post and went to find a doctor. He came back ten minutes later with Doctor Cadd, and after examining his patient, he said that with the medicine he had given her and with some good nursing, she should be on her way to recovery.

Mom breathed a sigh of relief, thanked the doctor and started to pay the bill. But when the money was offered, Doctor Cadd turned it down and told them it was only a little favor and he wouldn't take it. Dad thanked him and invited him to stay for supper, which he eagerly accepted, saying he didn't have a wife and was missing a good cooked meal; for he wasn't much of a cook and didn't like the food he made.

"Well, we'll be happy to have you," replied Dad, shaking his hand. "It's the least we could do."

----------

The next day, Martha was feeling much better, and the day after that she was nearly herself. And the journey to Colorado, continued.

# Chapter 6
## Emergency Stop

"I think Zoe will drop her foal tonight," announced Dad to Mom. "I think we should make camp earlier than usual and take two days off. We could all use a break, I think."

"Yes, I agree," replied Mom.

Upon hearing this news, the whole day brightened for Martha and there was a skip in her step as she helped her mother fix lunch. Martha read books and played puzzles with her sisters happily the rest of the afternoon.

They camped around four, and Martha went and fetched water again for supper and the dishes. An hour later, everyone was called to supper, and they all joined hands and prayed, "Dear Heavenly Father, thank You so much for protecting us on our journey thus far. Please help us to keep our trust in You. Thank You for this meal You have provided for us, and please bless the hands that made it and nourish this food to our bodies. Amen."

Everyone ate supper and then gathered around the fire as Dad read devotions. "*It is of the LORD's mercies that we are not consumed, because his compassions fail not. They are new every morning: great is thy faithfulness. The LORD is good unto them that wait for him, to the soul that seeketh him. It is good that a man should both hope and quietly wait for the salvation of the LORD."* Lamentations 3:22-24.

"Indeed, great is His faithfulness! Amen?" exclaimed Dad.

"Amen!"

"Let us try to wait patiently for Him and wait expectantly for His coming. Let's thank Him for His unwavering love and support."

They all bowed their heads as Dad prayed, "God, thank You so much for sending Your own Son as a baby to live on this sinful earth and to die on the cross for our sins. We should've been the ones on that cross. But He suffered Your wrath for us so that we might have a way to heaven. Thank You, God. Help us to wait patiently and expectantly for Your coming. In Jesus' Name we pray, amen."

"How about we sing 'Blessed Assurance'?" suggested Mom.

"Good idea, wife."

And the family raised their voices in chorus to the Maker of all things.

---------

Before long, it was time for bed. Martha didn't want to leave the cozy fire. She had a lot of things on her mind that she wanted to talk about. But, regretfully, she got up and helped undress her sisters, helped them into bed and got ready for bed herself. She could hear Dad talking to Mom as he finished his cup of coffee and knew that a long night was ahead for him.

---------

The next morning, Martha woke up with a start and wondered if Zoe had had her foal yet. She jumped out of the wagon and hurried to where Zoe was standing. Mom welcomed her and wrapped an arm around her. Martha looked and tried to see if a foal was with Zoe, but she couldn't see anything. She looked questioningly up at her Mom, but Mom just smiled mischievously at her and then looked at Dad.

Suddenly, hooves could be seen on the other side of the mare, and Martha quietly went around to see it. It was a pretty dark brown horse, who looked the spitting image of its mother, except it had a spot on its chest. "Is it a boy or girl, Daddy?"

Dad smiled at her and said it was a male. Martha returned his smile and asked, "Can I name it?"

"We'll see. Now, why don't you go and get dressed and start on your chores?"

"All right." Martha skipped back to the wagon.

After breakfast was eaten, Mom sent the boys down to the river to haul buckets of water, for she, Martha and Anna were going to wash the clothes that day. Martha wasn't looking forward to it as she gazed at the large pile of clothes that had to be washed. But she guessed it was better than walking and riding that day, so she vigorously started sorting the shirts, pants, and skirts out so they could do a load one at a time.

When the boys had filled up the tub, Mom started scrubbing the wash while Martha rinsed them and rung them in another bucket. They switched places after a while when Mom's hands got tired. Anna laid them on the grass to dry.

By noon, they had half of the wash done. The shirts and pants were lying on the grass drying, and they only had the skirts, socks, and underwear to do. Martha's arms ached from scrubbing, but she kept at it, knowing that the sooner it was done, the sooner she could play.

By the time they finished, it was time to start supper, and Martha knew she wouldn't have any free time that day. But she was happy that the wash was done and looked forward to the next day. She sat by the fire contentedly after devotions and gazed up at the stars. These were the same stars that Abraham looked at when God told him that He would make his descendants a great nation. She prayed and went to get ready for bed.

As she lay there, in her bed, she knew that Dad would be up a lot of the night, watching for wolves and other creatures that may try to come and harm the mare and the foal. As she said her prayers, she lifted up Zoe and the foal to God and asked that He might protect them through the night.

----------

The next morning, Martha helped her mother with breakfast and then sat down to eat. After the prayer was said, Dad exclaimed that he had an announcement. "To avoid any quarreling over what the foal's name would be, your mother and I have selected a name." Here he stopped, to make the suspense rise. "We have decided on the name 'Jerry' for him."

"I like the name Jerry," Thomas exclaimed and everyone agreed with him.

"Then welcome to the world, Jerry," said Dad in an exaggerated voice.

Later that morning, Martha helped her Mom make some loaves of bread. After lunch, being free to play, Martha called Nellie and they both ran down to wade in the cool water. Her other siblings were already down there, and what a time they all had splashing in the water.

# Chapter 7
## Perseverance

It was now the month of May. Mom and Lydia both celebrated their birthdays. Mom turned thirty-nine and Lydia turned six. On this certain morning, which was the 7th, Dad had an announcement to make.

"Family, I'm happy to say that we've made very good headway on our journey to Colorado. I'm proud of everyone's perseverance."

Everybody gave a cheer and Sarah spoke up, "Are we almost there, Daddy?"

"No, sweetie, we aren't. We still have quite a ways to go, but it's a start. Anyway, we'll be starting on our journey in half an hour, so let's huddle around and have our devotions."

After devotions, Dad hitched up Vernon and Zoe and made sure the foal's rope was secured to the back of the wagon, and the family started off.

Martha sighed and thought, *Bye home, and friends. For the first time, I feel like I'm on a deserted island and like we're the only ones in the world.* She pushed on with a weary heart, trying to find good in their moving, but her heart wasn't in it.

Suddenly, a hand slipped into hers and she looked down into the face of Elizabeth, who had come to her side. "Flower for you," and the two-year-old handed it up to Martha.

Martha took the pretty, yellow daisy gratefully, patted Elizabeth's cheeks and replied, "Thank you, dear sister. The flower is very pretty." And from that moment on, Martha felt encouraged.

Before long, the sun's warmth on the land grew warmer and warmer and Dad declared lunch and a short break.

Martha helped her mom with lunch, which was sandwiches and a jar of pickles for a treat. Everyone enjoyed the meal and then continued on.

Martha was looking around enjoying God's creation when she heard a noise. It sounded like a low grunt. She turned toward the sound and saw two buffalo fighting about thirty feet away from them. She pointed them out to Anna and Lydia who were walking beside her and then went on ahead to tell the others. Soon, the buffalo were out of sight and Martha tried to find something else interesting to look at.

Midway through the afternoon, Martha decided to sit in the wagon, for her feet were getting tired from walking. She hurried and jumped on the end and then crawled and settled herself on a pile of blankets and started reading. She yawned after a while and then took out her diary from a bag she had with her.

*May 7th, 1931*

*Dear God,*

*I am in the wagon right now so my handwriting won't be too good since my pencil is jostling around on the page, but I'll try my best. Today, I saw some buffalo fighting about thirty feet away. It was pretty cool.*

*God, thank You for giving me continual encouragement even when I don't deserve it. Elizabeth came to me today and handed me a flower as I was feeling down and discouraged. You're always comforting me in the smallest ways. But, often, the smallest things mean the MOST to me. So, I thank You. Please protect us on the rest of our journey. I'll try to write again soon!*

*Your Daughter and Servant,*

*Martha Rosemary Knight*

"There, I feel better now," she said and bowed her head to pray.

The next few days, the family traveled hard over the western terrain. On the fifth day, when they stopped and camped for the night, Martha saw Dad look worriedly over the peak of a mountain in the distance. Martha came up to him and asked, "Is everything all right, Dad?"

"Yes, I think so. It looks like we'll be getting some rain though. Hope it's not a lot. Well, I'd better go and feed the horses. I'll see you in a bit," Dad smiled at his daughter and headed off in Vernon and Zoe's direction.

Martha looked up toward the mountain and indeed saw clouds in the distance starting to form. The problem with rain was, if it soaked the ground too much and created a lot of mud, the wagon wheels would be mired down and that would cause a problem. People were stuck for days trying to dig out the wagon wheels before the mud hardened. She went to fetch some water for Mom, but a worried crease on her forehead could be seen the rest of the evening.

That night, as she lay in bed, she could hear the soft rumble of the thunder and see a few flashes of lightning, and soon, she could hear the pitter-patter of the rain on the canvas that covered the wagon.

----------

The next morning, the rain continued in a drizzle, but nothing much, and Martha was thankful for that. The wagon wheels hadn't sunk yet, and Dad was anxious to get an early start on their day. So, they hurried through breakfast, which was a meal of cold biscuits, and after Dad led them through devotions, they were on their way.

Since it was drizzling, everybody except Dad and the boys were in the wagon, and after a few hours of their trip, Sarah, Lydia, and Elizabeth were getting restless. So Martha suggested they play a game with some cards she had brought along with her.

Later, Martha plopped herself down near the end of the wagon, where she would still be sheltered from the rain, with her Bible in her lap. She watched Nellie, the faithful Pyrenees, as she trailed behind them with her sopping wet coat of hair. Martha felt sorry for her. She turned her head to see Jubilee napping in the box Martha had brought along to keep her in. She smiled and thanked God for two wonderful pets.

Martha opened her Bible to James 3:17-18.

"But the wisdom that is from above is first pure, then peaceable, gentle, and easy to be entreated, full of mercy and good fruits, without partiality, and without hypocrisy. And the fruit of righteousness is sown in peace of them that make peace."

Lord, Martha prayed, please give me wisdom to be pure, peace-loving, gentle, compliant, full of mercy and good fruits. Help me to be compliant and do everything without arguing or complaining, and please help me to have patience with my siblings. I thank You. In Jesus' name I pray, amen.

She continued to pray for her friends, Cathryn and Rose, Polly, Mary, as well as her new friend Francesca and her new found faith in the Lord Jesus. She prayed that He would keep Francesca's faith strong. She also prayed for the Kate family and rejoiced that they were able to move back to their home.

She had just finished her prayer when the wagon suddenly lurched forward and downward. The younger girls screamed and clung to each other while Martha and Mom grabbed the sides of the wagon to keep from falling.

When the wagon settled, everyone climbed out and went to the front and saw to their dismay that they were stuck in mud. The gooey substance was halfway up the horses' legs and Zoe was trying to pull back while Vernon just stood and tossed his head and neighed uneasily.

The front wagon wheels were stuck pretty deep and Thomas came up beside her and groaned.

"Rosemary, why don't you unpack lunch? I think we'll be here for the rest of the day trying to get out of this mud," said Dad.

Mom obeyed immediately and set to work preparing lunch while the boys cut down some strong, young trees to help maneuver the wagon out of the mud. Martha helped Mom and tried to keep the girls out of the mud puddles that were around. Finally, the lunch was ready and they all sat down to the meal.

Afterward, Dad and the boys got back to work. There wasn't much to do but sit around and watch them work. Mom worked on some schoolwork with the children and Martha pulled out her history book.

Martha sighed and prayed, *This is going to be a long day, Lord, but please help us to persevere in these trials and please, help Dad and the boys to get the wagon out of the mud soon!*

---------

Martha woke the next morning and looked over at the wagon. It was out of the mud!

"I see you got the wheel out," proclaimed Martha to her father who was sitting on a log with a cup of hot coffee.

"Yes, praise the Lord. We finally got it out late last night."

Martha smiled and got to work helping her mom with breakfast. When breakfast was ready, Martha helped Elizabeth change and buttoned Sarah's and Lydia's dresses, and then they all sat down to the meal of oatmeal with sugar.

Dad prayed, "Dear Lord, thank You for helping get us out of this mess so we could continue our travel. Lord, please nourish this food to our bodies, and please bless the hands that made it. Help us to serve You this day. Amen."

Everyone dug into the meal, and once the dishes were finished, Dad took out his Bible and started to read from it.

*"Ye are the light of the world. A city that is set on an hill cannot be hid. Neither do men light a candle, and put it under a bushel, but on a candlestick; and it giveth light unto all that are in the house. Let your light so shine before men, that they may see your good works, and glorify your Father which is in heaven."* (Matthew 5:14-16)

"What do you think these verses are telling us?" questioned Dad to his family.

Anna spoke up, "I think it means we need to be spreading the Word of God to everyone. We need to be that light on a hill so everybody can see it. We should let our light shine before men, so that they may see our good works and give glory to our Father in heaven."

"Very good, Anna, I want all of you to be memorizing this verse. Who knows, we may meet some people on the road who don't know the Lord, and we want to be a shining light to them. Let's sing: 'O, God Our Help In Ages Past'

*"O God our help in ages past, our hope for years to come!*
*Our shelter from the stormy blast and our eternal home!"*

The family left shortly afterwards and Martha walked alongside the wagon holding the hands of Elizabeth and Lydia.

Lydia was chatting happily to Elizabeth, but after a while they got bored, so Martha started to tell them a story to cheer them up. Later, as she laid down for sleep that night, Martha prayed for Irene and her family and thanked the Lord for providing such good friends that would allow them to stay with them while they built their house.

As she drifted off to sleep, she finished her prayer by saying, *God, please continue to protect us. I know that we have so many more miles to travel. Please protect us through whatever adventures You give us. In Jesus' name I pray these things, amen.*

# Chapter 8
## Weary of Travel

It was now May 28th and everyone was getting tired of traveling. Martha was trying to keep cheerful for her siblings' sake, but it was getting hard. However, it allowed her time to think and to pray and she was thankful for that.

Martha woke that morning with a slight headache and knew this was not going to be a good day, but determined to do her best, she prayed, got dressed and helped Mom with breakfast.

About an hour later, they were once more on the road. Martha overheard Dad saying to Mom that they would reach a town at noon that day, and Martha's heart leaped for joy.

*A town?!* thought Martha. Maybe she could play with some of the girls there, if there were any.

They reached the town in record time, and Mom gave her husband a list of the things they needed from the store while she and Martha set to work preparing the noon meal.

Martha kept her eyes peeled for any sign of children. She saw Thomas and James playing off in the distance with some of the boys that were in town, but she didn't see any girls. She determined that after lunch she would start a search.

Her belly stuffed with the good meal, Martha set off on her quest. There were quite a few houses around but she still didn't spot any girls in sight. Martha sighed and turned back to camp, deciding that she would take her sisters into the store to go window shopping. At least it was something to do.

Anna and Lydia set off with her eagerly, but Sarah and Elizabeth stayed behind, saying that they wanted to finish playing with their dolls.

Nellie trailed behind them and would have come into the store, but Martha told her to sit. They went into the store and the girls went right over and looked at all the dolls and the candy.

Martha felt sorry that she couldn't buy any candy, but to her complete surprise, the storekeeper gave them each a peppermint stick. The girls thanked the storekeeper for his generosity and they walked out of the store.

Martha suggested that they sit under a tree yonder so that Sarah and Elizabeth wouldn't see their candy. Martha commented to her sisters, "We aren't trying to hide our treats, but we don't want to show our candy off to the others when they don't have any."

The other girls nodded understandingly.

Anna sighed contentedly after she finished her candy. "That peppermint stick was really good."

"Yes, it was," seconded Lydia, sighing happily.

"Martha, may Lydia and I run over there to the stump to play tea party? We could run back to the wagon to get our dolls."

"Yes, you may. Just don't go any farther down. I'll go with you to get your dolls from the wagon."

"Great, thank you!" replied Anna as she and Lydia started toward the wagon.

After arriving back at the tree, Martha closed her eyes and thought what a wonderful day it was. It wasn't too hot and it wasn't too cold. She fell asleep to the sound of the wind in the grass and was unaware of the danger to her sisters.

Suddenly, she was awakened by the sound of a snarl. She sat up straight and turned her head to the noise, and she saw that there was a wolverine coming close to her sisters. The girls had climbed up on the stump and had their arms around each other, terrified.

Martha swallowed hard. She couldn't go over there or she would be stuck too. Then, she remembered something. Nellie hadn't left the store. She stayed to watch the boys. Martha ran to the store, and to her relief the big dog was still there. She called from about forty feet away. "Nellie, come!"

The dog hurried over and wagged her tail. Martha pointed in the girls' direction. "Go help Anna and Lydia!"

The dog rushed off with Martha right behind her. She decided to start screaming, as if to scare it off, but that pulled its attention to her, and the wolverine started toward her. Nellie barked and barred her teeth as if to give a warning.

Martha yelled, "Girls! I want you to run as fast as you can to the wagon and tell Dad to come quickly with his gun. Hurry!"

----------

Anna and Lydia started running toward the wagon and were out of breath by the time they reached it. Mom looked up and was frightened by the looks on the girls' faces. "What happened?" she asked, hugging the girls.

"Where's Dad?" Anna asked.

"He went to give the horses a drink. What's the matter?"

"There's a w-wolverine way over yonder, and it's after Martha! She has Nellie, but who knows if even she can stop that angry animal. Martha told us to run and get Dad to bring his gun," explained Anna.

"Well, we haven't any time to get Dad, so come on." Mom ran to the wagon to get Dad's gun.

Then, making sure Anna and Lydia were with her, she told them to keep ten feet behind her and to run if needed. They all set off at a run.

By the time they got there, Nellie and the animal were in a full-fledged fight. The wolverine, Mom noticed, was frothing at the mouth, and that convinced her that it had rabies. When she was about five feet away from the fight she cocked the gun and held it to her shoulder.

Her breathing came in rasps, and beads of sweat trickled down her forehead. She took a deep breath and let it out and prayed, "Dear Lord, help me make this shot," and POW! The gun went off, making her take a step backward because of the force on her shoulder.

She breathed a sigh of relief as she saw the wolverine totter for a moment and then fall dead on the ground. Martha ran toward her, put her arms around her neck and cried, "Oh, I was so scared, Mom! But, boy, are you a good shot. You hit him right on target. I was praying for you!"

"Thank you, Martha. I'm so glad you're safe. Come on. Let's go back to the wagon. Did the wolverine bite Nellie any?"

"No, I don't think so. It sure tried, but Nellie was quicker and was able to dodge him."

"That's a mercy, because I believe that animal had rabies."

"Really? God sure was protecting me and the girls. It was a wonder that Nellie was still at the store since the boys were gone."

"Yes, we need to thank God that He kept you safe and sound."

"Mom, can we pray right now?"

"Certainly, that's a great idea."

They clasped hands and bowed their heads as Mom led them in prayer. "Dear Heavenly Father, thank You for Your protection today. We are so very thankful that Martha, Lydia, and Sarah have been delivered from the danger without injury. Thank You for Your many blessings. We love You. In Jesus' name we pray, amen."

After supper, Martha felt bone tired and decided to retire after devotions. She got ready for bed, said her prayers and went to sleep, sending up another little prayer of thankfulness for her protection.

# Chapter 9
# Wyoming

The next week, Dad announced that they had made it to Wyoming. They were now half way to Colorado, and everyone let out a cheer of excitement.

"Girls, help your mother with the dishes and we'll be on our way."

"Yes, Dad," they replied.

As Martha put the last dish away, she thought, *We're a long way from home now. It never hit me this way before. I wonder what my friends are doing? Cara and Mary are probably helping their mother with the garden. Polly is probably doing her school. I sure do miss them. I wonder if I'll ever see them again?*

She carried the box of dishes over to the wagon, and a few minutes later, they set off. Martha could tell her dad was eager to make rapid progress through Wyoming. She sighed and looked back. "Farther and farther away from home we go."

----------

By the time they stopped for lunch, Martha was thoroughly exhausted and famished. Her dress was all sweaty and she felt hot and sticky, but she helped her mother with lunch and soon after they were on the road again. Martha climbed into the wagon, pulled out a book she was reading and settled down for the next two hours.

"Martha, I want a story," demanded Sarah, as Martha laid down her book.

"Can you say please?" Martha answered kindly.

"No, I don't want to say please," replied Sarah with a pout.

Just then, Dad's voice came through the wagon, "Sarah Knight, you will say please. It's a rule in this family that we use proper etiquette."

"What's that?"

"It means good manners. Now you repeat that question with a nice 'please'."

"All right," and Sarah turned to Martha, "would you please read me a book?"

"Yes, Sarah, I will."

She plopped down on Martha's lap. Martha groaned. She was so hot that she made Martha feel miserable. "Sarah, dear, would you please sit beside me? You're hot; so when you sit in my lap, you make me hotter."

"Sure, Martha," and she scooted off of Martha's lap and sat contentedly beside her sister with her thumb in her mouth.

About ten minutes later, Mom hopped on the wagon, followed by Lydia and Anna. "It's very hot out there. How would you like a snack?"

"I could use one about now, Mom. Thank you," replied Martha.

"All right, here's an apple, eat up."

"Thanks."

Martha munched into the apple, and after she was finished with her snack, laid down and decided to take a little nap.

"Martha...Martha, wake up."

Martha opened her eyes and found she was nose-to-nose with her sister Lydia. "What is it?" she asked.

There's a really scary man up ahead. I don't like him. Come see."

Martha rolled over and peered through a crack in the canvas covering the wagon. There was a man on horseback coming their way. He had black hair, with white streaks through it. He had a crude hat on and had an ugly scar on his chin. He was frowning.

"Well, hopefully he'll pass us on by without any trouble," Martha replied, fidgeting with the strings on her bonnet. She had read books with men like these, and it sure wasn't a comforting thought that this man might be dangerous.

*Perhaps he's an escaped criminal running from the authorities and he'll take us hostage!* Martha thought to herself but quickly shook her head. *No, that's silly.*

"Martha, bring me my gun," ordered Dad in a low voice so the approaching stranger couldn't hear.

"Yes, sir," Martha replied, as she quickly got up and hurried to get the requested weapon.

As Martha handed him the gun, he whispered to her, "Call the boys in from behind the wagon and keep all of them there until the stranger has passed."

Martha obeyed the order and called the boys up, then pulled the sleeping Elizabeth onto her lap and sat quietly.

Meanwhile, Dad was giving his wife orders to get inside the wagon if needed on his signal when the stranger rode up alongside them. "Good day," greeted Dad as he stopped the wagon.

"Huh, good day. What kind of a good day would you think this is?"

"Well, it is quite hot, but it's been a great day for us."

"Oh, really?" he said mischievously, narrowing his eyes.

"I'm sorry, sir, if you don't feel the same way."

"Huh, happy do-gooders."

He spurred his horse and rode to the back of the wagon and used the tip of his gun to move the blanket that covered the back. "You sure got a lot of children. I got one boy and he's the laziest and most no good boy you ever saw," he grinned, and then spat on the ground. "Yup, you's gots some good looking kids."

Dad got down from the wagon with his gun and came round to where the stranger was standing. "I'd appreciate it if you would please move on. You've said enough," said Dad, motioning with his gun toward the direction he was heading.

"Why shore! Don't see why you been so itchy, though."

"I'm sorry, but move on."

The stranger spurred his horse into a trot and Dad watched him disappear from sight. Then he turned around. "Is everyone okay?"

"Yes," answered James for all of them, "just a might scared. That's all."

"Well, you had a right to be. Let's move on and thank the Lord for protecting all of us."

----------

Later that night, as they stopped to camp, Martha helped Mom with supper and after devotions, Mom asked Martha to go down to the creek to get some water for washing the dishes. "Take Nellie with you and come right back when you've filled the bucket," commanded Mom.

"All right, come on, Nellie," Martha called to the big dog, and she came bounding up and they started off for the woods.

88

When they reached the creek, Martha knelt down to fill her bucket, and when she did, she heard a snap of a twig. *What was that?* Martha looked up and looked around the area, but didn't see a thing.

She got up and called to Nellie and found she had been sitting beside her all along. Martha thought, *Then who snapped the twig?* She looked around and finally said to herself that it was probably a squirrel eating its supper of nuts.

The sun had started to set and the shadows were lengthening. Thinking she better make haste to get back to the wagon before night fell, she took one more look around and starting walking briskly back to camp, all the while thinking, *Why should I feel afraid? I have Nellie with me and God's with me, too!*

She was almost out of the woods when she heard another twig snap and heard the crunching of leaves. Martha quickly turned about and found herself looking back into deep, dark woods.

*Calm down, Martha, there's nothing to be afraid of.* Martha quickened her steps to get back to camp. As she continued walking, she became even more frightened as she heard echoing footsteps behind her. She almost screamed with fright, but looked behind her, and this time saw a shadow of a hat, the same looking hat that she had seen on the stranger earlier that day. Had he followed them all this way, and what for?

Martha didn't want to find out so she quickly started at a run, dropping the bucket full of water. When she reached the camp, she was out of breath. Dad came to her side and asked what was wrong.

"There's...there's a...man in the woods, he...he looked like the same man we saw earlier...earlier today. I'm so scared. I'm sure he was following me!"

# Chapter 10
## Old Friends

Dad grabbed his gun and ran off toward the woods, telling his family to stay where they were. He left Mom with the loaded pistol that he had bought in the previous town. Mom gathered all the children together and tried to calm Martha down. James offered to play a game of checkers by the fire with Martha, which she consented to, and several minutes later, she found herself in victory against her brother. "You want to play again?" coaxed James, hoping for a rematch.

"No, James. Not right now. Thanks for playing with me though. You helped take my mind off my scary adventure. But I wonder why Dad's not back yet? It's been ten minutes, at least."

"I'm sure he'll be back soon," replied Mom, who had overheard the question. "I'm going to go put Elizabeth to bed in the wagon. I'll be right back."

She was not gone long and shortly after she was resuming her usual spot on the log by the fire. Everybody waited anxiously as an hour passed and no sign of Dad, an hour and a half passed and still nothing.

"Anna, Lydia, and Sarah, it's time for you to go to bed."

"Mom, can't we stay up until Dad gets back, please?" pleaded Anna.

"No, dear. There's no telling how long your father will be out there, so off to bed with you. Come here and I'll unbutton your dresses."

They did so, and kissing her goodnight, they headed off for their beds in the wagon. Martha went and got her history book to study and brought it by the fire.

"Boys, don't you have some math to do?" asked Mom.

"Yes, ma'am," replied both boys and they hurried off to find their math books.

"Mom," started Martha, "what do you suppose is keeping Dad so long?"

"I don't know, dear. Maybe he's talking with the stranger, but you know the Lord will take good care of him, and your father's not a careless man. He knows when to stop if there's much danger."

"You're right, Mom," and Martha turned back to her history book, but her thoughts were more on her absent father.

About twenty minutes later, Dad came back and reported that he couldn't find anybody, but said he would look again in the morning when he could see better. Martha said goodnight and headed off to bed, thanking the Lord for bringing her father back to her family safely.

----------

Meanwhile, Dad and Mom were having a talk. "Do you think it was that man we saw today, honey?" asked Mom.

"I don't know, but I think there's a good chance it was."

"I was worried when you were gone a long time."

"I'm sorry, sweetheart. I'm going to be extra careful around this area. There have been some thieves around here and I don't want them bothering us. That's why I bought the pistol back in the last town. So whenever I have to leave you and the children, you'll have something to defend yourself with. I'm really sorry you had to go through all this, darling."

"I know you are, and you've done a great job of protecting us and guiding us this whole way. I know the Lord will protect us. He always has and I know He always will. '*When thou passest through the waters, I will be with thee; and through the rivers, they shall not overflow thee: when thou walkest through the fire, thou shalt not be burned; neither shall the flame kindle upon thee.*'" Mom quoted the verses.

"God sure gave me a gift when He gave me you as a wife," replied Dad lovingly.

"Same here," replied his wife as she sat down on his lap and put her head on his shoulder.

----------

The next morning after breakfast, Dad and Martha headed off to the spot where she had spotted the man.

"It was about right here that I looked back and saw the shadow of the man's hat," said Martha.

Dad walked over to the tree indicated and looked. He knelt down and seemed to be studying something. Martha came over and looked over his shoulder. "Hoof prints!"

"Yes, and here are some human footprints as well. They look like they belonged to a man."

"Oh, Dad, I was so scared. What if it's the same man that we saw yesterday?"

"Well, I believe he's gone now, but from now on, I'm sending one of the boys with you. I'm sorry I didn't do it before. I don't want any of my children to get hurt. I think that man might have been out to rustle our horses."

"Rustle?" questioned Martha.

"Yes, rustlers are people who try to steal livestock. I wouldn't be surprised if he was going to try to rustle our horses."

"Wow," exclaimed Martha in amazement.

"Well, hopefully we'll have no more trouble. Let's head back to the wagon. We need to be starting again soon."

They started off and the rest of that day went without any scary, unusual events.

----------

The next day, they got an early start and by lunch time, they neared a house in the distance. They decided to ride up there and see if anybody lived in the house and if they could lunch there.

They arrived at the house shortly and found a little girl playing on the porch. When she saw them, she went into the house.

"Father, Mother, somebody's at the front door, come see." Martha could hear her excitedly exclaim to the adults inside.

The parents came and asked who they were and Dad said, "I'm sorry to disturb you. My name is Peter Knight and this is my wife, Rosemary. We wondered if we could luncheon here on your land? We won't give you any trouble."

"Knight. That name sounds familiar. Where have I heard it before...? Anyway, my name is Jeremiah Cube and this is my wife, Bethany. You're more than welcome to have your lunch here and why don't you come in and eat with us? We have plenty of food, don't we, hon?" replied Jeremiah Cube cheerfully, turning to his wife.

"We sure do; come on in."

"Are you sure we wouldn't be any trouble?" questioned Dad.

"Oh, no, you're fine."

"Well, thank you for the kind offer. We'd like to accept it."

Dad got down and helped Mom and then called to the children to come out. He introduced them, and after he finished, Mr. Cube looked at Martha and said, "I recognize your name from somewhere. I wonder if my brother mentioned it from when he was in Montana?"

"Mr. Cube, does your brother happen to be Matt Cube?"

"Yes, indeed," he replied.

"He worked for my father while he was searching for your father last fall."

"That's where I've heard your name before. Matt mentioned he had stayed with a family named Knight, and I do believe he mentioned a girl named Martha. He spoke highly of you."

"I think a lot of him, too," replied Martha, beaming with pleasure.

"Come on in. This is our daughter, Audra, and as you can see, we have another on the way." Jeremiah put a hand on his daughter's shoulder and motioned to his wife's bulging belly.

"Congratulations!" exclaimed Mom, as the family stepped into the house.

"You boys can put the horses in the barn, and there's feed in the bins on the east wall. It's on us," ordered Mr. Cube.

"That's very kind of you, but you don't have to do that," exclaimed Dad.

"No, no. I insist."

"All right."

"Hey, Dad," called Jeremiah, "guess who's here!"

Xavier Cube came in through another room, smiled and shook hands with Dad when he saw them. He exclaimed, "Good to see you! How are you?"

"Fine, how about you?"

"Doing great. I've enjoyed living with my sons and daughter-in-law."

"And me too, Grandpa," added Audra.

"And you too, darling."

Mom went to help Bethany in the kitchen and Martha and Sarah set the table. When lunch was on, the boys came in from the barn, bringing Matt with them.

"Hello, Mr. Knight, glad to see you out this way."

"Glad to see you too, Matt. Great to see your family doing so well."

"Yes, we're very blessed. What brings you way out here?" Matt questioned.

"I'll explain after prayer."

Everyone bowed their heads as Xavier said the prayer, adding an extra blessing upon the Knight family.

After everyone started eating, Dad explained that they were on their way to Colorado and told of the adventures they had had so far.

Sarah, Lydia, and Anna were having a great time talking with Audra, who had just turned four.

"Are you excited about your new brother or sister?" asked Anna.

"Oh, yes. I can't wait to start playing with him. I can't wait until he gets born. It's going to be sooo much fun."

"I remember when Elizabeth was born. She was so fun to play with, and she's still fun. She's only two," Anna remembered.

"Is she the youngest?"

"Yes, and Sarah's your age, and Lydia's six."

"That's great! Matt told me about you, Sarah. He said you were very nice," exclaimed Audra, turning to her young friend.

"I think he's very nice, too," exclaimed Sarah. "He told

"Yay!" everybody exclaimed. "Let's go play." me about you, too!"

After lunch, Dad announced that they had better go, but with a little persuasion from the Cubes, they decided to stay overnight.

"There's a nice creek down about a mile, come on. I'll race you all there," challenged Matt, bending down so Audra could jump up on his back. and with that, he raced out the door with six other people behind him. Soon, Thomas and James overtook him, and by the time they reached the creek, everyone was out of breath. Martha came in fourth and the three girls in last.

Everyone was laughing and having a good time. They took off their shoes and stockings and waded in the creek. Nellie, who had tagged along, splashed the water with her tail and barked. After a while the boys decided to make boats out of sticks and race them with the girls joining them. Martha and Matt sat together on the bank watching them.

100

"So, you're on your way to Colorado. I'm sure you miss your friends."

"Very much; more than I can say, but, I'm trying to trust the Lord with my life, and I am getting a little excited about getting closer to Colorado. I can't wait to see Irene again. It's not been quite a year since I last saw her. We've been writing a lot."

"I'm sure you have. What adventures have you had on your journey?"

Martha told him about the stranger and he agreed that the situation was kind of scary. "The Lord sure has protected me and my family the whole way that we've come. We're a long way from Montana now."

"Well, maybe you can go back someday, and it is pretty cool to be able to write to friends and see what they're up to."

"You're right, it is. But I think my favorite part is receiving the letters."

They both laughed at this and decided to join the others in their boat racing.

Everybody had a fine time at the creek, and by the time they were finished, it was nearly supper time and the group headed back up to the house, laughing and joking the whole way. Martha thought she hadn't had a nicer time in a long while.

# Chapter 11
# Waiting Patiently

The next morning, Martha found her sisters' bed empty. She heard laughter out the window so she assumed her sisters were already outside.

She dressed and hurriedly went out to join her sisters, and to her surprise she found Anna standing on the fence about to jump on Jerry's back!

"Anna, don't do that!" yelled Martha to her sister. Lydia was holding Jerry by his halter and trying to hold him still, but his ears were flattened back, signaling that he was mad.

But it was too late. Anna had just jumped on his back, Lydia let go of the halter and Jerry stood still for a few seconds, but then he started bucking.

"Hang on, Anna!" cried Martha as she ran full speed to the barn. Surely there was somebody in the barn doing the chores. She opened the door and Matt looked up from milking the cow. "Matt, hurry, Anna's on Jerry's back and I can't get her off!"

Matt got up from the stool, ran out of the barn, finding Anna crying on the ground, holding her arm. Matt and Martha knelt beside her and Martha exclaimed, "Anna, what a foolish thing to do! Whatever made you get on Jerry's back? He's too young and untrained. Are you okay, dearie?"

"I-I'm sorry. I was trying to be a cowgirl. But my arm really hurts."

Martha shook her head. Matt picked her up and carried her to the house and laid her on the couch, all while calling his sister, Bethany, and Mrs. Knight.

When Mom saw Anna sprawled out on the couch, she exclaimed, "What happened?"

"She was trying to ride on Jerry's back, but he bucked her off," said Martha.

"Anna Lillian Knight, what a crazy thing to do. A nine year old ought to know better than to try to ride on that foal's back. But are you okay?"

"That's what Martha said, my arm really hurts," replied Anna, wincing with pain.

"Mrs. Knight, I believe she needs a doctor. I'll go and get him."

"All right, thank you, Matt."

Matt got up and went to the barn to saddle the horse.

About a half hour later, the doctor arrived. He introduced himself as a Dr. Carly, and then he checked out Anna's arm and pronounced it broken. He put it in a splint, warning her, "This is going to ache some, young lady. I suppose this'll teach you to think before you do something like that again. But little girls usually heal quickly." He smiled as he got up and shook Mrs. Knight's hand. "You can take it off in six weeks and have it checked again by the nearest doctor. You may want to put ice on it to soothe the pain."

"All right, thank you, Doctor Carly. What do I owe you?"

"Nothing, it wasn't much."

"Are you sure?"

"Quite. Goodbye; nice meeting you!"

"Goodbye."

The next day they were on their way again. Martha was sad to leave behind her old friends, but was eager, as well, to be on the road, for it was not much longer until they would get to Colorado.

# Chapter 12
# Colorado

*June 15th 1931*

*Dear God,*

*We are now in Colorado. We crossed the border about three days ago. Colorado is very hilly and mountainous. Montana was the same way. I'm getting more excited as we near our destination. I can't wait to see Irene again and meet her brothers and sisters. I hope I can adjust quickly. It's not much different than back home, but it's just being in a different place.*

*I guess I don't handle change very well. I like things to stay the same. But, now that things have changed so much in the past three months, nothing looks familiar. I guess I need to learn to embrace it, because changes come and go as they please, whether I like it or not. The sun still rises and I always have to meet new mornings, new changes, new problems, and new adventures.*

*Your Daughter,*

*Martha Rosemary Knight*

Martha closed her diary, leaned back in the wagon, closed her eyes and dreamed of her friends. What would they be doing now? What changes might they be going through?

-----------

The next day, while Martha was cleaning up the dishes from lunch, Thomas came running up to her and exclaimed, "Come on, Martha. Look what we found!"

"All right," replied Martha, hurriedly putting the last dried dish into the box. Mom was working on laundry, since they had stopped for the rest of the afternoon. Mom called as Martha started off, "Martha, be back in half-an-hour."

"Yes, Mommy!" replied Martha, for they were already half way to the lake.

When they got there, Martha gasped in delight. "Oh! A rope swing to jump in the lake--how fun!"

"Daddy said we could go swimming, but we have to stay in the shallow end."

"Yay!" Martha joyfully shouted. "I haven't been swimming in ages." Martha grabbed onto the rope and was about to jump when James put a hand on her shoulder and asked, "Aren't you going to change into your swimsuit?"

"No, I'm just going to swim in my clothes this time," she explained. So her brother let go and she swung into the air and dropped off. She popped out of the water and sputtered, "Now, this is a kind of change I like."

"What?" asked Thomas, inquiringly.

"Oh, nothing," replied Martha.

"Here we come!" called out James, and he and Thomas jumped in with her.

A half hour passed and Martha had to head back up to camp. James and Thomas decided to come with her so they trooped on up. When they got to camp, Mom's eyes widened, "By the looks of you, you went swimming in the lake without something dry to put on," she laughed.

"Sorry, Mom, but at least these clothes are already clean," laughed Martha, going up and giving her mother a kiss. "I'll change clothes and be right out to help you wring out our wet things."

After Martha helped her Mom with the clothes, her sisters wanted her to play a game of Blind Man's Bluff with them. Of course, she was going to be it. So, after being blind folded and being spun in a circle about a dozen times, Martha dizzily tried to find her unseen sisters. Sometimes they would pull at her dress or poke her and she would whirl around and try to catch them, but most of the time with no success.

At the starting of the third game, Anna suggested that they spin Martha thirty times.

"Thirty times!" exclaimed Sarah, "I can't even count to thirty."

Martha quickly whipped the handkerchief off. "Sarah Knight, you do know how to count to thirty. I heard you counting to Mom," she said encouragingly.

"I guess I forgot about that. I guess I can try."

Martha put the blind fold back on and Anna spun her thirty times with her uninjured arm. When Anna let go of her, she nearly toppled, but then she heard a big growl, and then a roar. Her sisters screamed and Martha set off at a run. She couldn't get her blind fold off. Anna had tied it on GOOD!

She headed in the direction she thought was the way to the wagon. She heard her mom shouting something, but she was so dizzy that she couldn't focus correctly on what was being said.

All of a sudden, SMACK! She ran into something hard. She felt something trickle down her nose, down her lips and finally onto her chin and then she didn't know anymore.

----------

The next time Martha woke up, she was in the wagon with Mom gazing over her worriedly. "Oh, Martha, you gave us all quite a scare. You ran into a tree pretty hard."

"My head and my nose hurt."

"I know, honey. It's going to be bruised pretty badly. I'll get you some tea." She got up and went out to get the drink.

Thomas stepped through and said, "I'm sorry I scared you, Martha. I came up and growled and roared like a bear. I didn't think it would bother you. So, it's my fault that you're hurt."

Martha thought back, "So it wasn't a bear that scared me?" Then Martha got mad, "It could've been worse than it was. Go away, Thomas. I can't believe what a mean and dirty trick you pulled on me."

"Please forgive me Martha, I'm really sorry," replied Thomas, sincerely.

"Go!"

Martha heard his retreating steps and thought to herself that what she was doing wasn't right. The Lord said to forgive others as He forgave you. But Martha didn't want to forgive her brother. Because of him she would be bruised for several days. Martha closed her eyes and tried to think of something else, but as hard as she tried, she couldn't forget how she hadn't forgiven her brother. And it would hang over her like a dark rain cloud for days to come.

----------

The next few days were a pain to Martha. She had to ride in the wagon because her head hurt so badly and her nose was sensitive.

Martha avoided Thomas and stayed very bitter toward him. She knew she was handling the whole situation wrongfully and she was sinning, but she wasn't willing to repent.

Thomas was very distraught over his sister's avoidance of him. Mom encouraged him to leave the situation to Martha, suggesting she would eventually get over it. Mom knew her conscience would win over sometime. He stayed away from her to keep from anymore arguments. Mom also said to pray for his sister. She told him that the move had been just about the hardest on her, and she had a big weight on her shoulders that she was carrying. She was holding her feelings inside, and someday, they would all come out.

So, he persistently prayed for her and hoped that it wouldn't be much longer until he and Martha could reconcile with one another.

That day came about five days later when Martha was feeling much better and Mom had asked Thomas and her to go to the river and get a bucket of water. Martha was determined not to speak to him, so she headed off with her nose tipped up in the air and a haughty step.

Thomas kept up with her. It was a very awkward silence for him, so he decided to try to start a conversation.

"Hey, Martha, I'm really sorry for what I did and causing you to run into that tree. I've been praying that you would feel better soon. I know this move that we've made has really been hard on you and you're trying to be strong for the rest of us. I haven't heard a single complaint from you. You're the best older sister I know. Although you're the only big sister I have."

Martha was silent for a moment, thinking, *My brother has been praying for me when I was so mean to him. And just now he's said some of the nicest compliments I've heard in a long time.*

She slowed her step, tears filled her eyes and with emotion, she said, "Thomas, I'm sorry. I was so mean to you. I know you didn't mean to scare me that badly. I feel ashamed of the way I've behaved toward you, especially when you've been so nice to me. You're a great brother. You're right. This move has been really hard for me. I miss my friends and home terribly. Would you please forgive me?"

"Of course I forgive you, sis."

Martha gave him a hug and he generously returned it.

"Come on, let's hurry and get the water. I'll race you to the river," he hollered and sped off.

"Hey, no fair, you got a head start!" she retorted and raced after him.

When they got back with the water, Mom smiled and thought to herself, *They must have made it up with each other, for they seem to be friends again.*

Martha and her mom did the lunch dishes, and Martha told her what a mess she had made of herself and how ashamed she was. She had no right to treat her brother that way. But she said how loving and kind her brother was and how he forgave her right away.

"You certainly do have a wonderful and understanding brother, Martha."

"Yes I do, Mom," she replied.

That night, as the family gathered around for devotions, Dad asked Thomas to choose a hymn. He thought hard for a moment but then he decided on "Faith Is the Victory." So they started.

*"Encamped along the hills of light,*
*Ye Christian soliders rise*
*And press the battle ere the night*
*Shall veil the glowing skies.*
*Against the foe in vales below*
*Let all our strength be hurled;*
*Faith is the victory, we know,*
*That overcomes the world.*

*Faith is the victory! Faith is the victory!*
*O glorious victory That overcomes the world!*

After finishing the hymn, Dad said, "I'm going to read a verse in Isaiah 43.

*"'But now thus saith the LORD that created thee, O Jacob, and he that formed thee, O Israel, Fear not: for I have redeemed thee, I have called thee by thy name; thou art mine.'"*

"Those are very promising verses, aren't they? God wasn't only saying that to Jacob, to Israel, He was saying that to us. Not to be afraid of whatever He brings us. We can trust it's for our good, and He will never give us more than we can handle."

After devotions were done, Martha sought out her brother, Thomas, who was feeding the horses. He looked up when Martha called his name. "Hey, Thomas, thank you for that song; it was just what I needed to hear."

"You're welcome. I was trying to think of a song that would mean a lot to you."

"Well, it sure did. Thank you. You are a great brother."

Thomas beamed with pleasure. "Thank you, glad you liked it."

Martha was tired and ready to go to bed. After reading those verses again from Isaiah, she hummed herself to sleep.

*"Faith is the victory! Faith is the victory! O glorious victory That overcomes the World!"*

Martha went to sleep on those last few words, *"O glorious victory that overcomes the world."*

# Chapter 13
## Long Road Ahead

They were nearing their destination, but they were coming up on a big mountain and Dad wanted to get over it as quickly as possible. He hoped to be at the top by sunset and get down by sunset the next day. So, to do that, they left at the break of dawn. The nice thing about it was that it wasn't too hot as it had been the last three weeks.

There was a path that other wagons had previously followed, so Dad stuck right on it. He did not want to get lost in the mountains. It was quite a risk going up this steep incline with seven children and a wife, so he paired them up because he didn't want the little ones to wander off and fall down the steep side when they got higher.

Mom had Elizabeth. Martha had Sarah. Thomas had Lydia and James looked after Anna.

They had just broken for lunch in a grassy area on the mountain where a nice, cool breeze was blowing. It had a nice brook which Dad let the horses drink from, but he stayed nearby to keep an eye on them.

They had just finished lunch and Dad was going to go hitch up Vernon and Zoe, when three big rocks tumbled over the side of the cliff that was nearest them. Zoe and Vernon reared up and neighed. Jerry started off at a bolt and was running right toward the edge of the mountain!

James raced after him while Dad calmed the adult horses. He was nearing the drop off and James thought to himself, *I've got to stop him or he'll run off the side of the rock.*

As Jerry reached the precipice, he stiffened, neighing, and rolled his eyes. James had stopped so suddenly at the edge of the mountain that he was teetering. He was afraid he might drop off as he glimpsed the foal backing away from the edge. Martha spotted him, and when she saw he was about to fall over the edge, she gasped and grabbed her mom's arm, pointing.

Mom gasped, then got up and sprinted toward her son, yelling for Martha to watch the little ones.

Dad, noticing all of the commotion, quickly saw what was happening and ran to help his son.

"He's going to fall off the edge!" screamed Anna.

Martha hugged Anna. "It's going to be all right. Dad and Mom will get him."

Everyone watched as Dad closed the gap between himself and his son. Martha sighed with relief as she watched her father grab James' arm and steady him. *Thank You, God! That was close. Thank You for helping Dad and Mom.*

As Mom saw that her son was safe, she grabbed Jerry by the halter and Dad and Mom walked James back to the wagon. Dad was talking with James. "Next time, son, just call for help. That was dangerous. You could have fallen over the edge."

"Yes, Dad," replied James, who was looking very pale.

Anna went over and hugged her twin carefully, as not to further injure her broken arm, clinging to him like she would never let go. "I'm okay, sis," James comforted.

"I was so scared, James!" Anna exclaimed.

"I know. I was, too, but God was watching over me, and Dad and Mom helped me."

"I'm so glad."

"Me too!" James hugged his sister back and then turned to help Mom.

They were shortly on the road again and traveled on up the mountain. They camped that night at a sheltered peak. There was a supplies cabin at the top. Dad thought it was a hiker's cabin. He looked around and hollered, but nobody was there, so Dad built a fire, and as the sun set, everyone gathered round for a late supper and devotions.

After devotions were done, Mom suggested that she read to them from a book she had brought with her. It was a surprise. She'd found the book at a store they had passed early in their journey. She'd had a little money left, so she'd decided to buy the book to surprise her children when they were further on in their journey. The book was called, "The Swiss Family Robinson". Everyone squealed with delight over the new book, for that was a luxury now.

After reading for an hour, it was about eight o'clock and time for the younger ones to be put to bed. "Mom, would you read just a little longer, please?" pleaded Anna.

"No, honey. We have a big trek down the mountain tomorrow, and some little girls I know need to be put to bed."

"Please!" whined Anna.

"Anna, do not whine and complain. What does the Bible say about whining?"

"'*Do all things without murmurings and disputings...*' Philippians 2:14," replied Anna, respectfully.

"That's right, now off to bed with you."

Mom and Martha helped Lydia, Sarah, and Elizabeth into their nightgowns and got them tucked under the covers.

"Martha," asked Lydia as her sister tucked the covers up to her chin. "Yes, dearie?"

"I'm glad James didn't get killed when he almost flew over the mountain."

Martha smiled at her sister's wording that he 'flew' over the mountain, but replied, "I'm glad, too, Lydia."

"If James died, would he have gone to heaven?"

"Yes, I believe he would. He professes to be a Christian, and I've seen much fruit grow out of him in the last few years."

"What fruit? I didn't know James had fruit growing out of him. I wanna see the fruit."

"No, Lydia," Martha laughed, "it's not fruit you can see. It's spiritual fruit. It's how he's changing inwardly as a young man of God. The Bible says that you know a person by the fruit he or she produces."

"Do I grow fruit, too?"

"Yes, I think you do," replied Martha.

"What kind of fruit am I growing?" she asked, still puzzled.

"Well, think of it this way. We know the fruits of the Spirit are love, joy, peace, patience, kindness, goodness, faithfulness, gentleness, and self-control. When you show love to your brothers and sisters, that's showing good fruit. When you show kindness by helping Mom with the dishes when you're not asked to, that's showing good fruit as well. When you display any of the fruits of the Spirit with a loving and willing heart, you are showing fruit."

"I am?"

"You sure are."

"Good night, Martha, I love you," replied Lydia, snuggling under the covers, deep in thought.

"Good night, Lydia, I love you, too." Martha lowered the lamplight and climbed down from the wagon. James challenged her to a game of checkers. Martha quickly agreed and her brother set up the game.

----------

Martha could tell that her little sister had been affected by their conversation the night before. The next morning it was Sarah's turn to wash the dishes, but Lydia offered to do it for her, because she knew that Sarah didn't really like that chore. Martha could hear her humming as she did the dishes. Martha smiled to herself and continued to fold the blankets they had used that night.

They were on the road by six o'clock sharp, and it ended up being a nice day, so Martha took off the sweater she was wearing that morning and wrapped it around her waist.

Mom now had Sarah. Martha had Elizabeth. Thomas had Anna and James had Lydia. They continued on this way until lunch.

After a lunch of peanut butter and jelly sandwiches, Mom and Anna started packing up while Martha went to bring the horses back up from where they were drinking from a little brook. Suddenly, she realized that Elizabeth was nowhere to be seen. Her heart started beating wildly. She hoped her sister hadn't fallen off the edge. She looked around for her father. He wasn't in sight at the moment, so Martha thought she might be with him, but then he returned without Elizabeth.

Martha ran up to him panicking. "Dad, I can't find Elizabeth. She must've wandered off!"

"Let's search for her, then. We'll split up."

"All right," replied Martha.

They started off and met again after ten minutes of searching and still no Elizabeth. Martha wanted to start crying, but she knew that she couldn't do that. She prayed, "Dear God, please protect my baby sister. She doesn't understand the danger of this mountain. Please keep her out of harm."

Dad ran up to her just then. "You haven't found her yet, have you?"

"No, sir."

"Well, let's check the far side. She may have gotten over there, although I think it's unlikely, but let me tell you this, Martha, I'm disappointed in you. You were supposed to be watching over her, and you let her get away from you. I'm very worried about her."

"Yes, sir," replied Martha, meekly. She felt awful about what had happened. Last time something like this happened, she had gone off by herself to search for her sister and another young friend. She almost didn't make it back, but by the mercy of God she did, and she had to tell her parents where she was going for the next month as a punishment.

What a scrape she had gotten herself into now!

# Chapter 14
## When You Pass Through the Waters

Just then, Martha had a thought, maybe Nellie could find her. "Nellie!" called Martha. The big dog came bounding to her side, wagged her tail and attempted to lick her hand. Martha pulled it away quickly and found Elizabeth's favorite quilt that she always slept with. "Find her, girl, find Elizabeth!"

The dog sniffed the blanket and then bent her head down to the ground to gather her bearings. Suddenly, with tail up, she set off in the direction of several bushes. Martha knew that right behind them was a steep drop off.

She followed Nellie until they came to the edge of the bushes. Martha prayed that her sister was all right. Suddenly the bushes started moving and Elizabeth's head popped out, her face covered with berry juice!

"Berries!" she cried, holding out some to Martha.

Martha grabbed her sister and hugged her with relief. She was safe now. "I'm not going to let you get out of my sight again. You should know better than to go traipsing off without us, Elizabeth Kathleen Knight!"

Martha made sure that the berries that her sister had been eating were not poisonous. Thankfully, they were just fresh ripe raspberries. Martha had a thought, *Maybe before we leave, Anna and I could come back down here and pick some berries for dessert tonight.* Martha's mouth watered at the thought.

Well, let's go back and give everyone the good news."

After hearing the incident, Mom clutched her baby girl to her heart and scolded her for leaving, but showered her with kisses. Dad looked relieved with the outcome and said to his daughter, "Well done."

Martha bowed her head meekly and replied, "Thank you, sir."

Thomas, sensing something wasn't quite right between his father and sister, tagged along when Martha went to get the berries. He offered to help pick them. Mom watched Elizabeth closely as they prepared to head on in their journey.

"Is everything well, Martha? You seemed uncomfortable when Dad congratulated you on finding Elizabeth."

"Oh, Thomas! Everything's gone wrong. I let Elizabeth out of my sight, and when Dad and I couldn't find her, he sort of got mad at me for letting her escape. I know I deserved every bit of it, and I know he didn't mean it. He was just worried. But those words still hurt. I'm beating myself up a lot already. I feel really bad about the whole thing," replied Martha, popping a raspberry into her mouth.

"I'm sorry, sis. I'm sure Dad didn't mean to be quite that hard on you, but, as you said, I'm sure he was worried."

"Yes, I know. I guess I'm just frustrated at myself. If I had been keeping as close an eye on her as I should've, this wouldn't have happened. I just don't know how she escaped."

"Don't be too hard on yourself. This could've happened to anybody. I'm surprised no one saw her leave."

"Thank you, Thomas; I feel better. I see Mom and Dad are ready to go, so let's get these raspberries back to the wagon."

"All right. This was a great idea. We haven't had dessert in ages," he replied, grabbing one more berry and dropping it in his mouth.

"Thanks!" Martha grinned happily.

They hurried back to the wagon, where everyone got assigned a buddy, and Martha made sure she knew where Elizabeth was from that moment forward.

When they had made camp at the foot of the mountain on the other side, they had supper, devotions, and then Martha and Thomas got the little ones to bed.

While all the children were busy, Mom approached her husband. "Peter, is something troubling our eldest daughter? When you complemented her, she lowered her head bashfully and replied with a 'yes, sir' instead of the usual, 'yes, Dad.' Is something wrong?"

Dad sighed and replied to his wife, "I was awfully hard on her when Elizabeth was lost."

"What did you say to her?" queried Mom.

Dad related the conversation, and after he finished Mom exclaimed, "Ah, I see. I'm sure she was already beating herself up pretty well."

"And I made it worse. I didn't mean it the way it sounded but I know I hurt her by the look on her face. I knew the situation was wringing her heart already."

"I'm sure it was an accident, sweetheart. Our daughter has a very sensitive heart, as do all our children, I think, but I believe especially with the last time Elizabeth got lost and the consequences of that, she feels that she's lost our trust in her. She took it pretty hard."

"I know. When she's finished tucking in the younger ones, I'll talk to her and apologize."

"I'm glad," she said, coming over and hugging him. "I know you didn't mean it, and I'm proud of you."

"Do you know how much I love you, Mrs. Knight?"

"A lot, Mr. Knight."

"Dear Mrs. Knight, may I have a kiss?"

"Yes, you may, dear Mr. Knight," she replied, giving the requested kiss.

"Ah, here comes Martha," said Dad, looking at his daughter who had taken up a book and was reading by the fire.

"I'm going to check on the girls. I promised them a kiss goodnight."

"Very good, dear," he replied, smiling affectionately at her.

----------

"May I talk with you, my daughter?" asked Dad.

Martha looked up with surprise. "Certainly," she replied, making room for him on the log she was sitting on.

He took the offered seat and sighed. "Martha, I'm sorry for being so hard on you. I was really worried about our little baby girl, and I shouldn't have said those things to you. Will you please forgive me?"

"But, Dad, you had a right to say them. I was the one who was watching Elizabeth."

"I know, but I shouldn't have blamed you the way I did. I was quite surprised that she escaped the eyes of all of us."

"I forgive you, Dad," replied Martha, giving him a hug. "I still feel horrible about the whole thing. This is the second time I've let something like this happen."

"Well, we learn from our mistakes, but last time you just thought irrationally; you didn't get self-control. This time, it was just a case where your eyes weren't on her when she tottered off."

132

"Yeah, but everything seems to be my fault when something bad happens."

"Whoa there, daughter, don't let this turn into self-pity."

"Sorry, Dad."

"Well, what you said isn't true. Things just happen that we can't control. I love to be able to control how things go, like making sure no harm comes to my wife and children. When I can't do that, I get worried about the future. That's when I remind myself Who is in control and Who makes the decisions for our futures."

"I guess you're right, and I forgive you, if you'll forgive me for not watching Elizabeth."

"I have nothing to forgive. I know you were watching her, but it was one of those things. And I'm proud of you, daughter, for thinking quickly and getting Nellie on the job of finding her. I should've thought of that. And what's more, I want you to know that I still trust you the same as I did before all this happened, and even more."

"Thank you, Dad," replied Martha, with tears in her eyes.

"I love you, daughter. I can't say how proud I am of you."

"I love you too, Dad. You're the best dad in the whole wide world."

"Thank you for the compliment, but remember your true Father is in Heaven and loves you more than I ever could."

"I will, Dad. You're the best EARTHLY father in the world!"

"Thank you, dear." He put his arm around her and hugged her for a while before he sent her to bed.

----------

The next day was a trial, as Martha soon found out.

They were to cross a big river that morning, and it was unusual for it to be this high this time of year. Dad wasn't very worried about it. He knew Vernon and Zoe could get over it with the wagon, but he tied Jerry to the back so he would stay afloat and the current wouldn't carry him downstream.

After breakfast, they started out. Martha was holding Elizabeth, Thomas had Sarah and James had Lydia, while Anna sat between the boys.

When they were about half way across, there was a sudden drop off and Anna screamed, "What was that?"

"The horses are swimming now, pulling the wagon with them. The river must be higher than Dad thought," explained Mom.

"Will we be all right?" yelled Anna, over the roar of the river.

"I think so, but, Martha, take that water proof basket and be ready to put Elizabeth in it in case we have to swim."

Martha obeyed, but Anna was panicking. "But the younger girls don't know how to swim!"

"Anna, calm down!" yelled Martha over the noise, giving her sister a look that told her sister more than just 'calm down.' The younger girl settled down and squeezed her eyes shut.

Martha put a quilt in the bottom of the basket and laid Elizabeth in it. She took a piece of rope nearby and attached it to the basket so she could hold on to it.

She was praying that they wouldn't have to swim to shore, knowing how dangerous it was. Her brother, Thomas, was also praying that they wouldn't have to.

Suddenly, the dreadful order was made. Dad thought it best to bail out, for he was afraid that they might lose the whole wagon, and he wanted to ensure that his family would make it to shore instead of being tossed along the rocks and killed. Mom quickly gathered Sarah up, ordering Thomas to take Lydia, and James to watch Anna.

Martha was the first to go in. Holding to the rope tightly, the current was strong and she struggled against it. She made a few efforts toward the shore, but as the current hit her she flailed and was thrown on her back, and suddenly, she realized she wasn't holding onto the basket anymore!

She watched, horrified, as the basket headed downstream at a fast pace. Lydia laughed joyously and pointed at the basket, blissfully unaware that her baby sister was in it. "Mommy, look! There goes baby Moses in the basket!" remembering the favorite story.

Meanwhile Martha, her eyes wild with terror, looked around. She spotted Nellie and told her to get the basket. Nellie, quick to obey, swam rapidly to the desired item of her master. Martha was praying that the basket wouldn't hit the rocks as Nellie swam downstream. Mom was trying to get her other children ashore, praying that her baby wouldn't get lost downstream.

Finally, Nellie caught the rope in her teeth. As Martha caught up to the dog, she grabbed the rope and held on with the other hand to Nellie's back and the faithful dog pulled them to shore.

What a relief to be on terra firma once again! They had gotten quite a ways downstream. She couldn't see the wagon anymore.

Martha lifted the cover of the basket, hoping her sister was all right, and found her asleep! She must've fallen asleep with the rocking of the basket in the water. Martha knelt on the rocky shore and thanked the Lord that He had brought them safely through. Once she was done with her prayer of thankfulness, she picked up the basket and headed to the wagon.

Her family, which had made it to shore unharmed, as well as the wagon, was relieved to see their oldest and youngest daughters returned to them. They had another round of thanksgivings to God, the protector of all His children that love Him.

That night, Martha made sure that Nellie had more than a few scraps from supper.

## Chapter 15
## Arriving in Boulder, Colorado

*June 19th, 1931*

*Dear God,*

*We arrived in Boulder, Colorado today. Yay! Dad says only a few more days until we arrive at the Williams', which is about twenty miles east of here.*

*I'm kind of nervous to see Irene again. It has not been even a year yet since I saw her. I know I'll be fine, but I guess it's about meeting her family and friends. Will I fit in? Will I be that 'strange' girl in the group? Now, I know I shouldn't think that. I'm going to be fine. I just need to be myself.*

*Well, I had better close, Sarah is calling me!*

*Your Daughter,*

*Martha Rosemary Knight*

----------

The next morning, Dad was ready to go very early, so they packed up and started out on the mountainous terrain.

It was chilly in the early morning, but by lunch it was quite warm, so Martha took her sweater off and helped Mom prepare lunch. Before sitting down to have their meal, Dad checked to make sure no rattlesnakes were out on the rocks or in the high grass. Thankfully, he'd seen none, as of yet.

After lunch, the boys hitched Vernon and Zoe back up to the wagon, and the girls were busy doing the dishes. As Martha dried the last plate, she suddenly heard a loud, rattling, whirring sound. She turned and saw that Sarah was standing nearby the wagon watching the boys, and there was a rattlesnake not even five feet from where Sarah was standing.

Martha, struggling to stay calm, spotted Dad and called out, "Daddy, Sarah's in trouble! There's a rattlesnake near her and it could strike at any moment."

Both Dad and Thomas went to the aid of Sarah. Thomas spoke very softly to Sarah, "Sarah, I want you to very slowly walk toward me."

Sarah, terrified by the rattling snake, slowly shook her head. "I-I'm s-scared, Thomas!"

"I know, sweetie, but I need to you to come to me. Don't worry, just do as I tell you to and you should be okay."

Sarah nodded very slowly and took a very small step toward her brother.

"That's it, Sarah, just like that. You're doing great," encouraged Thomas as he held his arms out toward his sister.

Meanwhile, Dad had gone to get his gun. He was back now, just waiting for his daughter to move far enough so he could shoot the disturbed snake.

Just a minute later, Sarah made it to Thomas, and she fell into his arms and cried. "I was s-so scared, T-Thomas! Thank you for saving me!"

Thomas patted her back. "It's okay, Sarah, God was watching out for us, and He won't let ANYTHING happen to us that He hasn't allowed."

Sarah nodded as she wiped at her tears. Mom took her young daughter from Thomas and soothed her fears.

Martha came and stood next to her brother and put her hand on his shoulder. "I'm proud of you, Thomas."

"Thanks."

Just then, they heard a loud bang! Martha jumped a bit at the noise and turned to see the still wriggling snake, now dead. Dad turned to his youngest son. "James, go and get me a shovel, please."

"Yes, Dad," replied James, hurrying off to obey his father.

Martha turned back to where she had been washing the dishes and sent a prayer heavenward, *Oh, Lord, thank You for protecting Sarah and all of us. You are so good. Please keep us away from any harmful snakes on the rest of this trip and help Sarah to recover from her fright. In Jesus' name I pray, amen.*

They were soon back on the road, and the Knight siblings did their best to help Sarah forget about the snake incident.

# Chapter 16
## Arriving

They finally came to the Williams' ranch. It was in the distance, and Dad said it was about a mile ride over there.

Martha felt butterflies start to jump in her stomach, but she again rebuked herself. She was going to be fine. She would know Irene and she was very nice. Why was she nervous?

Just a few minutes later, they were nearing the ranch house. Martha could see a huge barn way off in the distance and cattle grazing in a far off field. Martha looked around for signs of anyone and finally saw a girl that looked to be about eleven years old. Martha guessed it was either Libby or Bealle.

When the girl spotted the wagon, she ran to the ranch house, and a few minutes later, Irene and her mom came out. Irene had a little boy that looked to be about four, by the hand.

Dad stopped the wagon and called, "Is this the Williams' ranch?"

"You've reached it, all right. You must be the Knight family. Irene has been telling me all about you. I'm Rachael Williams, and this is my daughter, Irene, and my youngest son, Trevor. Say hello, dear," she said to her little one.

Trevor waved shyly and then stepped behind his sister. Then, two identical twin girls came out holding hands. Mom smiled from her seat on the wagon and said, "Oh, you two must be the twins! Let me guess..." she thought for minute before pointing to the twin on the right, "You're Libby, and you're Bealle."

Libby shook her head with a smile. "No, I'm Libby, and she's Bealle," pointing to the left at her sister.

Mrs. Williams spoke back up, "That's okay, Rosemary, I used to do the same when they were quite young, and even now when I'm in a hurry, sometimes I'll get them mixed up."

She turned her attention to Mr. Knight. "Peter, you can put the horses in the barn. I would have my husband and oldest son do it, but they're out on the ranch checking the fences, but please, come on in," said Rachael with a kind smile.

Dad helped his wife down, shook hands with Rachael and turned and started to unhitch the horses. Thomas helped the girls down and Mom had them line up so she could introduce them. Then James and Thomas helped Dad put the horses away.

Martha hugged Irene, and her friend said, "Oh, Martha, I'm so glad you're finally here. You'll be staying with us while your house is being built. Come in and have a drink of water with me. It's getting late and Daddy and Allen will be getting home in the next hour. We were working on supper when you came."

"All right," replied Martha enthusiastically, her shyness slipping away.

"Can I help with anything?" asked Martha after their drink.

"No, not at all. You must be tired from all your traveling, so why don't you unpack? Bealle will show you to us girls' room."

"Okay," replied Martha, "I am kind of tired. Daddy was anxious to get here."

"I can only imagine," replied Irene, calling her sister into the kitchen.

Bealle showed Martha to their room and showed her where to put their things. Martha found the suitcases on the floor. Martha was surprised at how fast they got there. She set to putting away all the clothes and things, and when she had finished, she went downstairs and helped set the table. She could hear voices in the living room and guessed the other members of the Williams family had arrived.

After the table had been set and the food placed on the table, Irene called them for supper and everyone crowded in.

Mr. Williams and Allen, Irene's older brother, joined them. After they had washed up, Mrs. Williams introduced them. "Lee, Allen, this is the Knight family. Everyone, this is my husband, Lee, and my oldest son, Allen."

"Hello, Lee," exclaimed Mr. Knight, shaking Mr. Williams' hand, "it's nice to finally meet you in person."

"It's great to meet you guys," exclaimed Mr. Williams, pumping Peter Knight's hand up and down vigorously. "Now, introduce me to these children of yours."

Dad went through and introduced his children, oldest to youngest. After Martha had shaken Mr. Williams' hand, Allen came up and extended his hand to her. "It's nice to meet you, Martha. Irene has told us a lot about you."

Martha beamed with pleasure, "Well, it certainly is a pleasure to meet you as well. Thank you for letting us stay with you while our house is being built."

"It's our pleasure."

With a smile, Allen moved on to meeting Martha's other siblings.

They all sat down to the meal and Mr. Williams bowed his head to pray, "Dear Heavenly Father, thank You for this food You have provided for us. Let us be thankful. Please bless the hands that prepared it for us. In Jesus' Name we pray, amen."

Everyone started passing around fried chicken and fresh rolls. Rachael commented that they had no potatoes yet, for they were not ready to be harvested.

Mom smiled and said that was totally fine. "It's been so long since we've sat at a table that I'd be willing to eat almost anything!" she laughed.

Tears filled Martha's eyes. They hadn't been around a table since seeing Matt's family in Wyoming. She quickly blinked them away and looked around the table at her friend's family.

Allen looked like his father, with dark hair, but was different with his teasing blue eyes. Irene had blonde hair and wore it in a long pony tail on the back of her head and had sparkling, fun, dark blue eyes.

The twins, Libby and Bealle, had black hair with dark brown eyes. And little Trevor had blonde hair and a cowlick that ran down his forehead. He had blue eyes and looked more like his mother than anyone else.

Martha sighed, they looked so happy. Would she feel that happy ever again?

----------

After supper was finished and the dishes had been done by the twins, everyone gathered around for devotions, and at her request they sang one of Martha's favorite hymns at the end, "Trust and Obey."

*"When we walk with the Lord In the light of His Word, What a glory He sheds on our way! While we do His good will, He abides with us still, and with all who will trust and obey.*

*Trust and obey, For there's no other way To
be happy in Jesus, But to trust and obey.*

*Not a shadow can rise, Not a cloud in the
skies, But His smile quickly drives it away;
Not a doubt nor a fear, Not a sigh nor a tear
Can abide while we trust and obey.*

*Not a burden we bear, Not a sorrow we
share, But our toil He doth richly repay;
Not a grief nor a loss, Not a frown nor a cross
But is blest if we trust and obey.*

*Trust and obey, For there's no other way To
be happy in Jesus, But to trust and obey."*

After devotions, it was seven o'clock and
Elizabeth's eyelids started to droop, so Mom got up
and went to the guest room that Dad and she were
in and put Elizabeth in the crib that Rachael had
put in there for her.

Martha was sitting by Irene, who was
reading, and Libby and Anna were playing
checkers. Sarah, Lydia, and Bealle were playing
charades. Trevor was sitting by his mother's feet
putting together a puzzle and his dad, Lee, and Dad
were talking. Martha heard a little bit of their
conversation.

"We'll get your house up next week. I
announced in church that you would be arriving

soon, so I'll announce that the building will take place in the next week or so," said Lee.

"Are you sure it won't be any trouble? I could build us a home by myself. It would take longer, but that way I wouldn't be bothering anybody from their ranching."

"Are you kidding? We don't get many new families around these parts. It would be our pleasure. We can take some time off of ranching each day to help. Besides, most of the ranchers around here have older boys who can take care of everything at home."

"Well, I don't want to take them from their work," replied Dad, worried.

"Don't worry about it, Peter, your house won't take too long to build. With all of the men we have, we'll have your house up in a few weeks."

"But I don't have any money to pay them."

"They don't want your money. All they require is that you help somebody else when they come to Colderville."

"You've got a deal!" replied Dad, smiling and shaking Lee's hand.

"We'll start your house plans tomorrow. Do you plan to farm for a living? Honestly, the land here is not very fertile."

"Well, I did plan on it."

"If you want to start ranching, I could teach you the trade."

"That would be great. I'll talk with Rosemary about it tonight."

Martha sighed; her father seemed to be enthusiastic about ranching and starting over. Didn't he miss their home in Montana?

"Martha?" asked Irene, shaking her shoulder gently.

"Huh...I mean, yes?" she shook herself out of her thoughts.

"Are you ready to go to bed? We have a big day tomorrow."

"Oh, yes, that's fine."

"Are you all right, Martha?" asked Irene curiously.

"Yes, I'm fine, I was just thinking."

"About home?"

"Yes, I guess so," replied Martha, reluctantly.

"I know it must be hard for you, but hopefully, with some time, you'll come to think of here as your home."

"Maybe," but she thought: *I don't think so; nothing will ever be the same as living in Montana.*

Irene, Martha, and the other girls trooped up to the girls' big room.

"Wow!" exclaimed Lydia, "This room is huge. Our room wasn't this big back home."

All of the girls just chuckled.

Martha helped her sisters get into their nightgowns, and when they hopped into bed, Martha got ready herself and then opened her diary and wrote an entry there.

*June 28th, 1931*

*Dear God,*

*We arrived today and Irene is the same spunky, fun girl she was a year ago. I miss my friends terribly. Tonight, I heard Dad and Mr.*

*Williams talking about Daddy switching trades from farming to ranching; talk about a change!*

*I like things the old way. But I heard Mr. Williams say the ground here is not good for planting. So, oh well, I guess I have a lot of learning to do about change.*

*I've got to go to bed now. Irene says we have a big day ahead of us tomorrow. Time to learn about ranching!*

*Your Daughter,*

*Martha Rosemary Knight*

----------

The next morning, Irene woke Martha at about five o'clock, a full hour earlier than Martha usually woke back home. Martha looked around as Irene lit a lamp nearby. Libby and Bealle were already dressed and were putting their shoes on.

Martha yawned, hopped out of bed and quickly got dressed. She took out a dress from the closet, but Irene stopped her and said, "Around here we wear overalls while we work. I've got a pair you can borrow."

Martha hesitated, what would her mom think when she saw her? "...All right."

Martha borrowed an old farm shirt, slipped

into the overalls, put on her shoes and went downstairs where Rachael and Mom were already up making breakfast. Mom looked at her in surprise, but with a knowing look, she went back to stirring pancake batter.

Martha followed Irene out to the barn. The barn was mostly full of cows.

"I've never seen more cows in one barn in my life!" exclaimed Martha. "We had one cow back home we named Cassie, but we had to sell her."

Irene laughed and replied, "This is a dairy barn. We sell the milk at market every other day, and today is the every other day. We have ten cows." She went down the line naming them all, "Janny, Iona, Gwen, Bessie, Minnie, Minerva, Dana, Wendy, Era, Sandra."

That's a lot of cows!" exclaimed Martha, laughing along with her friend.

"Libby and Bealle are around here somewhere, so we had better get started; roll up your sleeves, sister!"

Irene said that Bealle did Janny, Iona and Gwen. Libby did Bessie, Minnie, and Minerva, and Irene usually took Dana, Wendy, Era, and Sandra. But since Martha was here to help, she would let Martha do Era and Sandra. They were already behind, so Martha quickly sat down and started milking. The milk went split-splat, split-splat in the bucket.

By seven o'clock they were done with their barn chores, which included: feeding the chickens, and feeding the cows and horses while the boys filled their water tanks and raked new hay into the stalls.

They hurried inside and cleaned up and found Martha's younger sisters and Trevor setting the table. Five minutes later, everyone sat down to eat.

----------

After morning devotions, Martha and Irene took the milk buckets and set them in box containers, and put a cover over each jug.

Allen hitched up the horses for them. "Martha, come meet the horses," he called, motioning for her to come.

Martha walked over. "They're such pretty horses," she exclaimed, admiringly.

"Aren't they? This one's Lily and beside her is Manny," he replied, proudly. "Dad's given them to me to train."

"Wow, you've done a good job so far," she complimented him as he helped his sister and then her up to the wagon.

"Thanks! Be careful, Irene," he replied.

"I will. Have a good day at the ranch, Allen."

"All right, thanks," he replied, starting toward the barn.

It took them about a half hour to get to town, and Martha exclaimed, "It didn't take you long to get to town. Back in Montana, it took us half a day just to get to town, and by the time we got back, it was nearing supper time."

Irene stopped the horses next to the market and went inside. Martha followed her. Inside was a tall man with graying hair. He was speaking to a customer, so they waited patiently. When the customer left, the clerk said, "Ah, Irene, here to deliver the milk?"

"Yes, sir."

"I'm kind of busy here, so I'll have my apprentice Timothy help you. Timothy! Come here; got some customers for you."

Timothy, who looked to be about seventeen years of age, came from the back room and said, "What can I do for you two ladies?"

"We're here with the milk. If you'll just unload it, I'm taking Martha here for a surprise treat."

"All right, Miss Irene."

Irene lightly took Martha's elbow and went out the door. "Where are you taking me?" asked Martha, perplexed.

"There's a drug store down the road here. Mama gave me some money to buy two ice cream cones."

"Really?" squealed Martha in delight.

"Really," assured Irene.

"Wow. I usually don't have ice cream before lunch," giggled Martha.

"Don't worry; I asked our moms before leaving for town."

The bell jingled as the girls walked in, and an older lady stepped out from the back room and greeted the girls with a smile, "What shall I get for you young ladies today?"

"Hello, Ms. Hartford. Two ice cream cones, please," requested Irene, as the two girls came to the counter and sat on the chairs provided.

"All-righty, now, who might this girl be? I don't recall seeing her before."

"This is my friend, Martha. Her family has come all the way from Montana to make a living here."

"Is that so? Well, Martha, welcome to the community," said a beaming Ms. Hartford.

"Thank you, ma'am. We didn't have a drugstore in the town I lived in."

"Well, now, I hope your first experience here will be a happy one," the lady replied, handing the cones to the girls.

"Thank you."

After finishing their cones, Irene and Martha picked up the wagon and headed home. When they arrived at the Williams' ranch, Irene unhitched the horses, led them back to their stalls and cooled them off. Then they went into the house for lunch, which was at eleven.

It was wash day; so, after lunch, the girls went to gather all the clothes while Mom and Rachael boiled the water and got the wringer out. When everything was ready, the girls dumped the white clothing in one tub and the colored clothing in another tub and the girls started scrubbing furiously.

About an hour later, their mothers were busy wringing out the clothes and Anna and Lydia hung them while Sarah, Elizabeth, and Trevor were down for their naps.

By four o'clock, all the clothing was up drying, and Irene went in to change into a dress and apron and helped the women make supper. Martha, meanwhile, went to help the twins bring the hay out for the cattle on what Libby called field Number Two.

The girls went into the barn and brought out two huge horses. Martha's mouth gaped open and she exclaimed, "They're huge!"

"They're Clydesdales. This is Freddy and this is Meg," replied Bealle, pointing at each Clydesdale in turn.

"I've heard about those kinds of horses, but I never thought they would be so big."

The twin girls smiled at each other.

"Aren't they dangerous?" asked Martha.

"They can be, just like any horse, but Freddy and Meg are just as gentle as lambs. They wouldn't hurt anybody."

The girls hitched them up, with the help of their dads, who had returned to get something from the barn. After that task was finished, they got up on the wagon and headed toward the field.

It took about twenty minutes to get there. The girls could see Allen out in the field with the herd, and when they reached him, Libby handed the reins to Martha and said, "Hold these."

Martha took the reins nervously. What if the horses decided to bolt? What a mess she would be in.

Libby and Bealle jumped down and called to Allen, who replied, "You're just in time." He rode his horse, Blake, over to the end of the tall wagon and suddenly the hay just dumped out.

"How'd you do that?" asked Martha.

Allen had that teasing look in his eye. "It's a secret."

Martha narrowed her eyes at him, but Bealle answered her. "There is a rope at the end of the wagon and if you pull it, the back end of the wagon goes down and dumps the hay. But it takes someone strong to pull it."

"Like me!" said Allen, flexing his muscles.

Martha rolled her eyes. She hoped this new boy wasn't such a big tease as he was making out to be right now.

Soon, they were back at the house, and Libby and Bealle worked together to successfully unhitch the horses and drag their harnesses to the proper place. A nervous Martha washed them down and at last found out that they were really gentle; there was nothing to be afraid of.

That night, as Martha got ready for bed, Irene came in and started talking to her from the other side of the curtain.

"So, how are my cousins doing?"

"They're doing fine. Timothy is growing fast, and Kathy is the cutest thing. I think everything is going well for them."

"Good," replied Irene, starting to get ready for bed.

"Irene, do you remember the Kate family? They had a little girl named Jane."

"Yes, she was at the party that my cousins had last summer--a real nice girl."

"Yes, well, they moved to town that fall; for they were worried that they would have to leave because they didn't have enough money to survive the winter. Mr. Kate wanted to be ready to leave town that spring."

"That's too bad. This depression is getting worse and worse."

Martha nodded. "Perhaps her dad was able to find another job, though."

"That would be great," Irene replied, but sensed that her friend was kind of thinking out loud. "Martha, I know you miss your friends, but I have some great ones here, and I think you'll grow to be great friends with them soon."

"I guess, Irene, but it's hard for me to accept change."

"I've guessed that. But I know things will get better. I just know they will," replied Irene, getting into bed.

"I hope so, Irene. I really hope so," replied Martha beside her.

## Chapter 17
## End of Journey

The next few days went by quickly, and on Thursday, Martha needed a break. So, making sure it was okay with Irene and her mom if she walked down to the river for an hour, she grabbed her bonnet and tied it under her chin. As she stepped into the hot afternoon, Trevor stopped her by asking, "Where are you going?"

"Down to the creek."

"Can I come with you?"

"No, not this time, Trevor; I need some time by myself to think."

"All right, I have chores anyway."

"Goodbye," Martha called and headed toward the river.

She reached the desired spot in roughly ten minutes. She found a rock to sit on and opened her Bible which she had brought with her. She opened it to Lamentations 3:22-24, which read,

*It is of the LORD's mercies that we are not
consumed, because his compassions fail not. They
are new every morning: great is thy faithfulness.
The LORD is my portion, saith my soul; therefore
will I hope in him.*

Martha sighed and thought about the whole
journey here. They'd had a few tough scrapes, but
the Lord had been faithful to get them through
those scrapes without much damage. But why did
they have to move to this place? Why did God move
her away from all her friends and everything that
was familiar to her? Why, why, why?

There were a lot of 'whys' that Martha
couldn't explain. How could this place be home to
her? Dad had announced yesterday that he felt the
Lord leading him to start ranching. This was so
different from farming.

Martha put a hand to her head in an attempt
to slow down all the thoughts that were rushing
through her head. Then, a familiar song came to
mind that they would sing at church when they
were in Montana. She started singing it to herself
quietly,

*"Great is Thy faithfulness, O God my Father;
There is no shadow of turning with Thee.
Thou changest not; Thy compassions, they fail
not. As Thou hast been Thou forever wilt be.*

*Great is Thy faithfulness! Great is Thy faithfulness! Morning by morning new mercies I see; All I have needed Thy hand hath provided. Great is Thy faithfulness, Lord, unto me!*

*Summer and winter, and spring time and harvest, Sun, moon and stars in their courses above, Join with all nature in manifold witness To Thy great faithfulness, mercy and love.*

*Pardon for sin and a peace that endureth, Thy own dear presence to cheer and to guide. Strength for today and bright hope for tomorrow-Blessings all mine with ten thousand beside!*

*Great is Thy faithfulness! Great is Thy faithfulness! Morning by morning new mercies I see; All I have needed Thy hand hath provided. Great is Thy faithfulness, Lord, unto me!*

Martha thought about those words, especially, "strength for today and bright hope for tomorrow," and started praying. "Lord, please give me strength for today and help me to only think about what is in front of me, not what tomorrow may bring or the next. I just need to go one day at a time. Thank You that 'Thou changest not; Thy compassions, they fail not' and for all the blessings You give to us. I love You Lord, amen."

Martha got up and headed toward the house. It was time to take the hay out to the cattle again, and Libby and Bealle promised her they would let her hitch up Freddy and Meg, the Clydesdales.

----------

That night, before Martha went to bed, she opened her diary and got her pencil out and started writing:

*July 1st, 1931*

*Dear God,*

*This trip for me has been a whirlwind of changes, but I guess I need to learn to embrace change. I went out to the river today to think and You reminded me of Your faithfulness and also reminded me that You never change, no matter how much the world changes, my friends change, or, even how much I change; and for that I am most grateful.*

*I need to write my friends soon to tell them we've made it safely and tell them about our trip. I've been so busy learning about ranch life that I haven't had the time to.*

*Well, I'm getting tired and I need to go to bed. Thank You for protecting us on our journey and I can't wait to see what new adventures You have for me and mine!*

*Your Daughter,*

*Martha Rosemary Knight*

**The End!**

Will Martha learn to accept change?

Will she ever call Colderville, Colorado home?

Find out in book five:

<u>Martha's Sowing Season</u>

Made in the USA
Middletown, DE
19 April 2016